The Joyous Story of Toot

Laura E. Richards

The Joyous Story of Toto

CHAPTER I

TOTO was a little boy, and his grandmother was an old woman (I have noticed that grandmothers are very apt to be old women); and this story is about both of them. Now, whether the story be true or not you must decide for yourselves; and the child who finds this out will be wiser than I.

Toto's grandmother lived in a little cottage far from any town, and just by the edge of a thick wood; and Toto lived with her, for his father and mother were dead, and the old woman was the only relation he had in the world.

The cottage was painted red, with white window-casings, and little diamond-shaped panes of glass in the windows. Up the four walls grew a red rose, a yellow rose, a woodbine, and a clematis; and they all met together at the top, and fought and scratched for the possession of the top of the chimney, from which there was the finest view; so foolish are these vegetables.

Inside the cottage there was a big kitchen, with a great open fireplace, in which a bright fire was always crackling; a floor scrubbed white and clean; a dresser with shining copper and tin dishes on it; a table, a rocking-chair for the grandmother, and a stool for Toto. There were two bedrooms and a storeroom, and perhaps another room; and there was a kitchen closet, where the cookies lived. So now you know all about the inside of the cottage. Outside there was a garden behind and a bit of green in front, and three big trees; and that is all there is to tell.

As for Toto, he was a curly-haired fellow, with bright eyes and rosy cheeks, and a mouth that was always laughing.

His grandmother was the best grandmother in the world, I have been given to understand, though that is saying a great deal, to be sure. She was certainly a very good, kind old body; and she had pretty silver curls and pink cheeks, as every grandmother should have. There was only one trouble about her; but that was a very serious one,—she was blind.

Her blindness did not affect Toto much; for he had never known her when she was not blind, and he supposed it was a peculiarity of grandmothers in general. But to the poor old lady herself it was a great affliction, though she bore it, for the most part, very cheerfully. She was wonderfully clever and industrious; and her fingers seemed, in many ways, to see better than some people's eyes. She kept the cottage always as neat as a new pin. She was an excellent cook, too, and made the best gingerbread and cookies in the world. And she knit—oh! how she *did* knit!—stockings, mittens, and comforters; comforters, mittens, and stockings: all for Toto. Toto wore them out very fast; but he could not keep up with his grandmother's knitting. Clickety click, clickety clack, went the shining needles all through the long afternoons, when Toto was away in the wood; and nothing answered the needles, except the tea-kettle, which always did its best to make things cheerful. But even in her knitting there were often trials for the grandmother. Sometimes her ball rolled off her lap and away over the floor; and then the poor old lady had a hard time of it groping about in all the corners (there never was a kitchen that had so many corners as hers), and knocking her head against the table and the dresser.

The kettle was always much troubled when anything of this sort happened. He puffed angrily, and looked at the tongs. "If *I* had legs," he said, "I would make some use of them, even if they *were* awkward and ungainly. But when a person is absolutely *all* head and legs, it is easy to understand that he should have no heart."

The tongs never made any reply to these remarks, but stood stiff and straight, and pretended not to hear.

But the grandmother had other troubles beside dropping her ball. Toto was a very good boy,—better, in fact, than most boys,—and he loved his grandmother very much indeed; but he was forgetful, as every child is. Sometimes he forgot this, and sometimes that, and sometimes the other; for you see his heart was generally in the forest, and his head went to look after it; and that often made trouble. He always *meant* to get before he went to the forest everything that his grandmother could possibly want while he was away. Wood and water he never forgot, for he always brought those in before breakfast. But sometimes the brown potatoes sat waiting in the cellar closet, with their jackets all buttoned up, wondering why they were not taken out, as their brothers had been the day before, and put in a wonderful wicker cage, and carried off to see the great world. And the yellow apples blushed with anger and a sense of neglect; while the red apples turned yellow with vexation. And sometimes,—well, sometimes *this*sort of thing would happen: one day the old lady was going to make some gingerbread; for there was not a bit in the house, and Toto could *not* live without gingerbread. So she said, "Toto, go to the cupboard and get me the ginger-box and the soda, that's a good boy!"

Now, Toto was standing in the doorway when his grandmother spoke, and just at that moment he caught sight of a green lizard on a stone at a little distance. He wanted very much to catch that lizard; but he was an obedient boy, and always did what "Granny" asked him to do. So he ran to the cupboard, still keeping one eye on the lizard outside, seized a box full of something yellow and a bag full of something white, and handed them to his grandmother. "There, Granny," he cried, "that's ginger, and *that's* soda. Now may I go? There's a lizard—" and he was off like a flash.

"Oh, oh! what a dreadful face he made!"

Well, Granny made the gingerbread, and at tea-time in came Master Toto, quite out of breath, having chased the lizard about twenty-five miles (so he said, and he ought to know), and hungry as a hunter. He sat down, and ate his bread-and-milk first, like a good boy; and then he pounced upon the gingerbread, and took a huge bite out of it. Oh, oh! what a dreadful face he made! He gave a wild howl, and jumping up from the table, danced up and down the room, crying, "Oh! what *nasty* stuff! Oh, Granny, how *could* you make such horrid gingerbread? Br-r-rr! oh, dear! I never, never, *never* tasted anything so horrid."

The poor old lady was quite aghast. "My dear boy," she said, "I made it just as usual. You must be mistaken. Let me—" and then *she* tasted the gingerbread.

Well, she did not get up and dance, but she came very near it. "What does this mean?" she cried. "I made it just as usual. What can it be? Ah!" she added, a new thought striking her. "Toto, bring me the ginger and the soda; bring just what you brought me this afternoon. Quick! don't stop to examine the boxes; bring the same ones."

Toto, wondering, brought the box full of something yellow, and the bag full of something white.

His grandmother tasted the contents of both, and then she leaned back in her chair and laughed heartily. "My dear little boy," she said, "you think I am a very good cook, and I myself think I am not a very bad one; but I certainly can*not* make good gingerbread with mustard and salt instead of ginger and soda!"

Toto thought there *were* some disadvantages about being blind, after all; and after that his grandmother always tasted the ingredients before she began to cook.

Now, it happened one day that the grandmother was sitting in the sun before the cottage door, knitting; and as she knitted, from time to time she heaved a deep sigh. And one of those sighs is the reason why this story is written; for if the grandmother had not sighed, and Toto had not heard her, none of the funny things that I am going to tell you would have happened. Moral: always sigh when you want a story written.

Toto was just coming home from the wood, where he had been spending the afternoon, as usual. As he came round the corner of the cottage he heard his grandmother sigh deeply, as if she were very sad about something; and this troubled Toto, for he was an affectionate little boy, and loved his grandmother dearly.

"Why, Granny!" he cried, running up to her and throwing his arms round her neck. "Dear Granny, why do you sigh so? What is the matter? Are you ill?"

The grandmother shook her head, and wiped a tear from her sightless eyes. "No, dear little boy!" she said. "No, I am not ill; but I am very lonely. It's a solitary life here, though you are too young to feel it, Toto, and I am very glad of that. But I do wish, sometimes, that I had some one to talk to, who could tell me what is going on in the world. It is a long time since any one has been here. The travelling pedler comes only once a year, and the last time he came he had a toothache, so that he could not talk. Ah, deary me! it's a solitary life." And the grandmother shook her head again, and went on with her knitting.

Toto had listened to this with his eyes very wide open, and his mouth very tight shut; and when his grandmother had finished speaking, he went and sat down on a stone at a little distance, and began to think very hard. His grandmother was lonely. The thought had never occurred to him before. It had always seemed as natural for her to stay at home and knit and make cookies, as for him to go to the wood. He supposed all grandmothers did so. He wondered how it felt to be lonely; he thought it must be very unpleasant. *He* was never lonely in the wood.

"But then," he said to himself, "I have all my friends in the wood, and Granny has none. Very likely if I had no friends I should be lonely too. I wonder what I can do about it."

Then suddenly a bright idea struck him. "Why," he thought,—"why should not my friends be Granny's friends too? They are very amusing, I am sure. Why should I not bring them to see Granny, and let them talk to her? She *couldn't* be lonely then. I'll go and see them this minute, and tell them all about it. I'm sure they will come."

Full of his new idea, the boy sprang to his feet, and ran off in the direction of the wood. The grandmother called to him, "Toto! Toto! where are you going?" but he did not hear her. The good woman shook her head and went on with her knitting. "Let the dear child amuse himself as much as he can now. There's little enough amusement in life."

But Toto was not thinking of his own amusement this time. He ran straight to the wood, and entered it, threading his way quickly among the trees, as if he knew every step of the way, which, indeed, he did. At length, after going some way, he reached an open space, with trees all round it. Such a pretty place! The ground was carpeted with softest moss, into which the boy's feet sunk so deep that they were almost covered; and all over the moss were sprinkled little star-shaped pink flowers. The trees stood back a little from this pretty place, as I said; but their long branches met overhead, as they bent over to look down into—what do you think?—the loveliest little pool of water that ever was seen, I verily believe. A tiny pool, as round as if a huge giant had punched a hole for it with the end of his umbrella or walking-stick, and as clear as crystal. The edge of the pool was covered all round with plants and flowers, which seemed all to be trying to get a peep into the clear brown water. I have heard that these flowers growing round the pool had become excessively vain through looking so constantly at their own reflection, and that they gave themselves insufferable airs in consequence; but as this was only said by the flowers which did *not* grow near the pool, perhaps it was a slight exaggeration. They were certainly very pretty flowers, and I never wondered at their wanting to look at themselves. You see I have been in the wood, and know all about it.

It was in this pretty place that Toto stopped. He sat down on a great cushion of moss near the pool, and began to whistle. Presently he heard a rustling in the tree-tops above his head. He stopped whistling and looked up expectantly. A beechnut fell plump on his nose, and he saw the sharp black eyes of a gray squirrel peering at him through the leaves.

"Hello, Toto!" said the squirrel. "Back again already? What's the matter?"

"Come down here, and I'll tell you," said Toto.

The squirrel took a flying leap, and alighted on Toto's shoulder. At the same moment a louder rustling was heard, among the bushes this time, a sound of cracking and snapping twigs, and presently a huge black bear poked his nose out of the bushes, and sniffed inquiringly. "What's up?" he asked. "I thought you fellows had gone home for the night, and I was just taking a nap."

"So we had," said Toto; "but I came back because I had something important to say. I want to see you all on business. Where are the others?"

"Well," said Toto, "it's about my grandmother."

"Coon will be here in a minute," answered the bear. "He stopped to eat the woodchuck's supper. Chucky was so sound asleep it seemed a pity to miss such an opportunity. The birds have all flown away except the wood-pigeon, and she told me she would come as soon as she had fed her young ones. What's your business, Toto?" and Bruin sat down in a very comfortable attitude, and prepared to listen.

"Well," said Toto, "it's about my grandmother. You see, she—oh! here's Coon! I'll wait for him." As he spoke, a large raccoon came out into the little dell. He was very handsome, with a most beautiful tail, but he looked sly and lazy. He winked at Toto, by way of greeting, and sat down by the pool, curling his tail round his legs, and then looking into the water to see if the effect was good. At the same moment a pretty wood-pigeon fluttered down, with a soft "Coo!" and settled on Toto's other shoulder.

"Now then!" said the squirrel, flicking the boy's nose with his tail, "go on, and tell us all about it!"

So Toto began again. "My grandmother, you see: she is blind; and she's all alone most of the time when I'm out here playing with all of you, and it makes her lonely."

"Lonely! What's that?" asked the raccoon.

"I know what it is!" said the bear. "It's when there aren't any blueberries, and you've hurt your paw so that you can't climb. It's a horrid feeling. Isn't that it, Toto?"

"N-no, not exactly," said Toto, "for my grandmother never climbs trees, anyhow. She hasn't anybody to talk to, or listen to; nobody comes to see her, and she doesn't know what is going on in the world. That's what she means by 'lonely.'"

"Humph!" said the raccoon, waving his tail thoughtfully. "Why don't you both come and live in the wood? She couldn't be lonely here, you know; and it would be very convenient for us all. I know a nice hollow tree that I could get for you not far from here. A wild-cat lives in it now, but if your grandmother doesn't like wild-cats, the bear can easily drive him away. He's a disagreeable fellow, and we shall be glad to get rid of him and have a pleasanter neighbor. Does—a—does your grandmother scratch?"

"No, certainly not!" said Toto indignantly. "She is the best grandmother in the world. She never scratched anybody in her life, I am sure."

"No offence, no offence," said the raccoon. "*My* grandmother scratched, and I thought yours might. Most of them do, in my experience."

"Besides," Toto went on, "she wouldn't like at all to live in a hollow tree. She is not used to that way of living, you see. Now, *I* have a plan, and I want you all to help me in it. In the morning Granny is busy, so she has not time to be lonely. It's only in the afternoon, when she sits still and knits. So I say, why shouldn't you all come over to the cottage in the afternoon, and talk to Granny instead of talking here to each other? I don't mean *every* afternoon, of course, but two or three times a week. She would enjoy the stories and things as much as I do; and she would give you gingerbread, I'm sure she would; and perhaps jam too, if you were *very* good."

"What's gingerbread?" asked the bear. "And what's jam? You do use such queer words sometimes, Toto."

"Gingerbread?" said Toto. "Oh, it's—well, it's—why, it's *gingerbread*, you know. You don't have anything exactly like it, so I can't exactly tell you. But there's molasses in it, and ginger, and things; it's good, anyhow, very good. And jam—well, jam is sweet, something like honey, only better. You will like it, I know, Bruin.

"Well, what do you all say? Will you come and try it?"

The bear looked at the raccoon; the raccoon looked at the squirrel; and the squirrel looked at the wood-pigeon. The pretty, gentle bird had not spoken before; but now, seeing all the other members of the party undecided, she answered quietly and softly, "Yes, Toto; I will come, and I am sure the others will, for they are all good creatures. You are a dear boy, and we shall all be glad to give pleasure to you or your grandmother."

The other creatures all nodded approval to the wood-pigeon's little speech, and Toto gave a sigh of relief and satisfaction. "That is settled, then," he said. "Thank you, dear pigeon, and thank you all. Now, when will you come? To-morrow afternoon? The sooner the better, I think."

The raccoon looked critically at his reflection in the water. "Chucky bit my ear yesterday," he said, "and it doesn't look very well for making visits. Suppose we wait till it is healed over. Nothing like making a good impression at first, you know."

"Nonsense, Coon!" growled the bear. "You are always thinking about your looks. I never saw such a fellow. Let us go to-morrow if we are going."

"Besides," said Toto, laughing, "Granny is blind, and will not know whether you have any ears or not, Master Coon. So I shall expect you all to-morrow. Good-by, all, and thank you very much." And away ran Toto, and away went all the rest to get their respective suppers.

CHAPTER II.

"GRANNY," said Toto the next day, when the afternoon shadows began to lengthen, "I am expecting some friends here this afternoon."

"Some friends, Toto!" exclaimed his grandmother in astonishment. "My dear boy, what friend have you in the world except your old Granny? You are laughing at me."

"No, I am not, Granny," said the boy. "Of course you are the *best* friend, very much the best; but I have some other very good ones. And I have told them about your being lonely," he went on hurriedly, glancing towards the wood, "and they are coming to see you this afternoon, to talk to you and tell you stories. In fact, I think I hear one of them coming now."

"But *who are they?*" cried the astonished old woman, putting her hand up at the same time to settle her cap straight, and smoothing her apron, in great trepidation at the approach of these unexpected visitors.

"Oh," said Toto, "they are—here is one of them!" and he ran to meet the huge bear, who at that moment made his appearance, walking slowly and solemnly towards the cottage. He seemed ill at ease, and turned frequently to look back, in hopes of seeing his companions.

"Grandmother, this is my friend Bruin!" said Toto, leading the bear up to the horrified old lady. "I am very fond of Bruin," he added, "and I hope you and he will be great friends. He tells the most *delightful* stories."

Poor Granny made a trembling courtesy, and Bruin stood up on his hind-legs and rocked slowly backwards and forwards, which was the nearest approach he could make to a bow. (N. B. He looked so very formidable in this attitude, that if the old lady had seen him, she would certainly have fainted away. But she did not see, and Toto was used to it, and saw nothing out of the way in it.)

"Your servant, ma'am," said the bear. "I hope I see you well."

Granny courtesied again, and replied in a faltering voice, "Quite well, thank you, Mr. Bruin. It's—it's a fine day, sir."

"It is indeed!" said the bear with alacrity. "It is a *very* fine day. I was just about to make the same remark myself. I—don't know when I have seen a finer day.

In fact, I don't believe there ever *was* a finer day. A—yesterday was—a—*not* a fine day. A—

"Look here!" he added, in a low growl, aside to Toto, "I can't stand much more of this. Where is Coon? He knows how to talk to people, and I don't. I'm not accustomed to it. Now, when I go to see *my* grandmother, I take her a good bone, and she hits me on the head by way of saying thank you, and that's all. I have a bone somewhere about me now," said poor Bruin hesitatingly, "but I don't suppose she—eh?"

"No, certainly not!" replied Toto promptly. "Not upon any account. And here's Coon now, and the others too, so you needn't make any more fine speeches."

Bruin, much relieved, sat down on his haunches, and watched the approach of his companions.

The raccoon advanced cautiously, yet with a very jaunty air. The squirrel was perched on his back, and the wood-pigeon fluttered about his head, in company with a very distinguished-looking gray parrot, with a red tail; while behind came a fat woodchuck, who seemed scarcely more than half-awake.

The creatures all paid their respects to Toto's grandmother, each in his best manner; the raccoon professed himself charmed to make her acquaintance. "It is more than a year," he said, "since I had the pleasure of meeting your accomplished grandson. I have esteemed it a high privilege to converse with him, and have enjoyed his society immensely. Now that I have the further happiness of becoming acquainted with his elegant and highly intellectual progenitress, I feel that I am indeed most fortunate. I—"

But here Toto broke in upon the stream of eloquence. "Oh, *come*, Coon!" he cried, "your politeness is as bad as Bruin's shyness. Why can't we all be jolly, as we usually are? You need not be afraid of Granny.

"Come," he continued, "let us have our story. We can all sit down in a circle, and fancy ourselves around the pool. Whose turn is it to-day? Yours, isn't it, Cracker?"

"No," said the squirrel. "It is Coon's turn. I told my story yesterday."

"You see, Granny," said Toto, turning to his grandmother, "we take turns in telling stories, every afternoon. It is *such* fun! you'd like to hear a story, wouldn't you, Granny?"

"Very much indeed!" replied the good woman. "Will you take a chair, Mr.—Mr. Coon?" she asked.

"Thank you, no," replied the raccoon graciously. "My mother earth shall suffice me." And sitting down, he curled up his tail in a very effective manner, and looked about him meditatively, as if in search of a subject for his story.

"My natural diffidence," he said, "will render it a difficult task, but still—"

"Oh yes, we know!" said the squirrel. "Your natural diffidence is a fine thing. Go ahead, old fellow!"

At this moment Mr. Coon's sharp eyes fell upon the poultry-yard, on the fence of which a fine Shanghai cock was sitting. His face lighted up, as if an idea had just struck him. "That is a very fine rooster, madam!" he said, addressing the grandmother,—"a remarkably fine bird. That bird, madam, reminds me strongly of the Golden-breasted Kootoo."

"And what is the Golden-breasted Kootoo?" asked the grandmother.

The raccoon smiled, and looked slyly round upon his auditors, who had all assumed comfortable attitudes of listening, sure that the story was now coming.

"The story of the Golden-breasted Kootoo," he said, "was told to me several years ago by a distinguished foreigner, a learned and highly accomplished magpie, who formerly resided in this vicinity, but who is now, unhappily, no longer in our midst."

"That's a good one, that is!" whispered the wood chuck to Toto. "He ate that magpie about a year ago; said he loved her so much he couldn't help it. What a fellow he is!"

"Hush!" said Toto. "He's beginning!"

And Mr. Coon, dropping his airs and graces, told his story in tolerably plain language, as follows:—

THE GOLDEN-BREASTED KOOTOO.

Once upon a time—and a good time it was—there lived a king. I do not know exactly what his name was, or just where he lived; but it doesn't matter at all: his kingdom was somewhere between Ashantee and Holland, and his name sounded a little like Samuel, and a little like Dolabella, and a good deal like Chimborazo, and yet it was not quite any of them. But, as I said before, it doesn't matter. We will call him the King, and that will be all that is necessary, as there is no other king in the story.

This King was very fond of music; in fact, he was excessively fond of it. He kept four bands of music playing all day long. The first was a brass band, the second was a string band, the third was a rubber band, and the fourth was a man who played on the jews-harp. (Some people thought he ought not to be called a band, but he said he was all the jews-harp band there was, and that was very true.) The four bands played all day long on the four sides of the grand courtyard, and the king sat on a throne in the middle and transacted affairs of state. And when His Majesty went to bed at night, the grand chamberlain wound up a musical-box that was in his pillow, and another one in the top bureau-drawer, and they played "The Dog's-meat Man" and "Pride of the Pirate's Heart" till daylight did appear.

One day it occurred to the King that it would be an excellent plan for him to learn to sing. He wondered that he had never thought of it before. "You see," he said, "it would amuse me very much to sing while I am out hunting. I cannot take the bands with me to the forest, for they would frighten away the wild beasts; and I miss my music very much on such occasions. Yes, decidedly, I will learn to sing."

"Take this man and behead him!" said the King.

So he sent for the Chief Musician, and ordered him to teach him to sing. The Chief Musician was delighted, and said they would begin at once. So he sat down at the piano, and struck a note. "O King," he said, "please sing this note." And the King sang, in a loud, deep voice, The Chief Musician was enchanted. "Superb!" he cried. "Magnificent! Now, O King, please to sing *this* note!" and he struck another note: The King sang, in a loud, deep voice, The Chief Musician looked grave. "O King," he said, "you did not quite understand me. We will try another note." And he struck another: The King sang, in a loud, deep voice, The Chief Musician looked dejected. "I fear, O King," he said, "that you can never learn to sing." "What do you mean by that, Chief Musician?" asked the King. "It is your business to teach me to sing. Do you not know how to teach?" "No man knows better," replied the Chief Musician. "But Your Majesty has no ear for music. You never can sing but one note."

At these words the King grew purple in the face. He said nothing, for he was a man of few words; but he rang a large bell, and an executioner appeared. "Take this man and behead him!" said the King. "And send me the Second Musician!"

The Second Musician came, looking very grave, for he had heard the shrieks of his unhappy superior as he was dragged off to execution, and he had no desire to share his fate. He bowed low, and demanded His Majesty's pleasure. "Teach me to sing!" said His Majesty. So the Second Musician sat down at the piano, and tried several notes, just as the Chief Musician had done, and with the same result. Whatever note was struck, the King still sang,

Now the Second Musician was a quick-witted fellow, and he saw in a moment what the trouble had been with his predecessor, and saw, too, what great peril he was in himself. So he assumed a look of grave importance, and said solemnly, "O King, this is a very serious matter. I cannot conceal from you that there are great obstacles in the way of your learning to sing—" The King looked at the bell. "But," said the Second Musician, "they can be overcome." The King looked away again. "I beg," said the Second Musician, "for twenty-four hours' time for consideration. At the end of that time I shall have decided upon the best method of teaching; and I am bound to say this to Your Majesty, that if you learn to sing—" "What?"said the King, looking at the bell again. "That when you learn to sing," said the Second Musician hastily,—"*when* you learn to sing, your singing will be like no other that has ever been heard." This pleased the King, and he graciously accorded the desired delay.

Accordingly the Second Musician took his leave with great humility, and spent all that night and the following day plunged in the deepest thought. As soon as the twenty-four hours had elapsed he again appeared before the King, who was awaiting him impatiently, sitting on the music-stool. "Well?" said the King. "Quite well, O King, I thank you," replied the Second Musician, "though somewhat fatigued by my labors." "Pshaw!" said the King impatiently. "Have you found a way of teaching me to sing?" "I have, O King," replied the Second Musician solemnly; "but it is not an easy way. Nevertheless it is the only one." The King assured him that money was no object, and begged him to unfold his plan. "In order to learn to sing," said the Second Musician, "you must eat a pie composed of all the singing-birds in the world. In this way only can the difficulty of your having no natural ear for music be overcome. If a single bird is omitted, or if you do not consume the whole pie, the charm will have no effect. I leave Your Majesty to judge of the difficulty of the undertaking."

Difficulty? The King would not admit that there was such a word. He instantly summoned his Chief Huntsman, and ordered him to send other huntsmen to every country in the world, to bring back a specimen of every kind of singing-bird. Accordingly, as there were sixty countries in the world at that time, sixty huntsmen started off immediately, fully armed and equipped.

After they were gone, the King, who was very impatient, summoned his Wise Men, and bade them look in all the books, and find out how many kinds of singing-birds there were in the world. The Wise Men all put their spectacles on their noses, and their noses into their books, and after studying a long time, and adding up on their slates the number of birds described in each book, they found that there were in all nine thousand nine hundred and ninety-nine varieties of singing-birds.

They made their report to the King, and he was rather troubled by it; for he remembered that the Second Musician had said he must eat every morsel of the pie himself, or the charm would have no effect. It would be a *very* large pie, he thought, with nine thousand nine hundred and ninety-nine birds in it. "The only way," he said to himself, "will be for me to eat as little as possible until the huntsmen come back; then I shall be very hungry. I have never been *very* hungry in my life, so there is no knowing how much I could eat if I were." So the King ate nothing from one week's end to another, except bread and dripping; and by the time the huntsmen returned he was so thin that it was really shocking.

At last, after a long time, the sixty huntsmen returned, laden down with huge bags, the contents of which they piled up in a great heap in the middle of the courtyard. A mountain of birds! Such a thing had never been seen before. The mountain was so high that everybody thought the full number of birds must be there; and the Chief Cook began to make his preparations, and sent to borrow the garden roller from John the gardener, as his own was not big enough to roll out such a quantity of paste.

The King and the Wise Men next proceeded to count the birds. But alas! what was their sorrow to find that the number fell short by one! They counted again and again; but it was of no use: there were only nine thousand nine hundred and ninety-eight birds in the pile.

The next thing was to find out what bird was missing. So the Wise Men sorted all the birds, and compared them with the pictures in the books, and studied so hard that they wore out three pairs of spectacles apiece; and at last they discovered that the missing bird was the "Golden breasted Kootoo." The chief Wise Man read aloud from the biggest book:—

"The Golden-breasted Kootoo, the most beautiful and the most melodious of singing birds, is found only in secluded parts of the Vale of Coringo. Its plumage is of a brilliant golden yellow, except on the back, where it is streaked with green. Its beak is—"

"There! there!" interrupted the King impatiently; "never mind about its beak. Tell the Lord Chamberlain to pack my best wig and a clean shirt, and send them after me by a courier; and, Chief Huntsman, follow me. We start this moment for the Vale of Coringo!"

"He rode on horseback, and was accompanied only by the Chief Huntsman and the jews-harp band."

And actually, if you will believe it, the King *did* start off in less than an hour from the counting of the birds. He rode on horseback, and was accompanied only by the Chief Huntsman and the jews-harp band, the courier being obliged to wait for the King's best wig to be curled.

The poor Band had a hard time of it; for he had a very frisky horse, and found it extremely difficult to manage the beast with one hand and hold the jews-harp with the other; but the King, with much ingenuity, fastened the head of the horse to the tail of his own steady cob, thereby enabling the musician to give all his attention to his instrument. The music was a trifle jerky at times; but what of that? It was music, and the King was satisfied.

They rode night and day, and at length arrived at the Vale of Coringo, and took lodgings at the principal hotel. The King was very weary, as he had been riding for a week without stopping. So he went to bed at once, and slept for two whole days.

On the morning of the third day he was roused from a wonderful dream (in which he was singing a duet with the Golden-breasted Kootoo, to a jews-harp accompaniment) by the sound of music. The King sat up in bed, and listened. It was a bird's song that he heard, and it seemed to come from the vines outside his window. But what a song it was! And what a bird it must be that could utter such wondrous sounds! He listened, too enchanted to move, while the magical song swelled louder and clearer, filling the air with melody. At last he rose, and crept softly to the window. There, on a swinging vine, sat a beautiful bird, all golden yellow, with streaks of green on its back. It was the Golden-breasted Kootoo! There could be no doubt about it, even if its marvellous song had not announced it as the sweetest singer of the whole world. Very quietly, but trembling with excitement, the King put on his slippers and his flowered dressing-gown, and seizing his gun, he hastily descended the stairs.

It was early dawn, and nobody was awake in the hotel except the Boots, who was blacking his namesakes in the back hall. He saw the King come down, and thought he had come to get his boots; but the monarch paid no attention to him, quietly unbolted the front door, and slipped out into the garden. Was he too late? Had the bird flown? No, the magic song still rose from the vines outside his chamber-window. But even now, as the King approached, a fluttering was heard, and the Golden-breasted Kootoo, spreading its wings, flew slowly away over the garden wall, and away towards the mountain which rose just behind the hotel. The King followed, clambering painfully over the high wall, and leaving fragments of his brocade dressing-gown on the sharp spikes which garnished it. Once over, he made all speed, and found that he could well keep the bird in sight, for it was flying very slowly. A provoking bird it was, to be sure! It would fly a little way, and then, alighting on a bush or hanging spray, would pour forth a flood of melody, as if inviting its pursuer to come nearer; but before the unhappy King could get within gunshot, it would flutter slowly onward, keeping just out of reach, and uttering a series of mocking notes, which seemed to laugh at his efforts. On and on flew the bird, up the steep mountain; on and on went the King in pursuit. It is all very well to *fly* up a mountain; but to crawl and climb up, with a heavy gun in one's hand, and one's dressing-gown catching on every sharp point of rock, and the tassel of one's nightcap bobbing into one's eyes, is a very different matter, I can tell you. But the King never thought of stopping for an instant; not he! He lost first one slipper, and then the other; the cord and tassels of his dressing-gown tripped him up, so that he fell and almost broke his nose; and finally his gun slipped from his hold and went crashing down over a precipice; but still the King climbed on and on, breathless but undaunted.

At length, at the very top of the mountain, as it seemed, the bird made a longer pause than usual. It lighted on a point of rock, and folding its wings, seemed really to wait for the King, singing, meanwhile, a song of the most inviting and encouraging description. Nearer and nearer crept the King, and still the bird did not move. He was within arm's-length, and was just stretching out his arm to seize the prize, when it fluttered off the rock. Frantic with excitement, the King made a desperate clutch after it, and—

PART II.

At eight o'clock the landlady knocked at the King's door. "Hot water, Your Majesty," she said. "Shall I bring the can in? And the Band desires his respects, and would you wish him to play while you are a-dressing, being as you didn't bring a music-box with you?"

Receiving no answer, after knocking several times, the good woman opened the door very cautiously, and peeped in, fully expecting to see the royal nightcap reposing calmly on the pillow. What was her amazement at finding the room empty; no sign of the King was to be seen, although his pink-silk knee-breeches lay on a chair, and his ermine mantle and his crown were hanging on a peg against the wall.

The landlady gave the alarm at once. The King had disappeared! He had been robbed, murdered; the assassins had chopped him up into little pieces and carried him away in a bundle-handkerchief! "Murder! police! fire!!!!"

In the midst of the wild confusion the voice of the Boots was heard. "Please, 'm, I see His Majesty go out at about five o'clock this morning."

Again the chorus rose: he had run away; he had gone to surprise and slay the King of Coringo while he was taking his morning chocolate; he had gone to take a bath in the river, and was drowned! "Murder! police!"

The voice of the Boots was heard again. "And please, 'm, he's a sittin' out in the courtyard now; and please, 'm, I think he's crazy!"

Out rushed everybody, pell-mell, into the courtyard. There, on the ground, sat the King, with his tattered dressing-gown wrapped majestically about him. An ecstatic smile illuminated his face, while he clasped in his arms a large bird with shining plumage.

"Bless me!" cried the poultry-woman. "If he hasn't got my Shanghai rooster that I couldn't catch last night!"

The King, hearing voices, looked round, and smiled graciously on the astonished crowd. "Good people," he said, "success has crowned my efforts. I have found the Golden-breasted Kootoo! You shall all have ten pounds apiece, in honor of this joyful event, and the landlady shall be made a baroness in her own right!"

"But," said the poultry-woman, "it is my Shang—"

"Be still, you idiot!" whispered the landlady, putting her hand over the woman's mouth. "Do you want to lose your ten pounds and your head too? If the King has caught the Golden-breasted Kootoo, why, then it *is* the Golden-breasted Kootoo, as sure as I am a baroness!" and she added in a still lower tone, "There hasn't been a Kootoo seen in the Vale for ten years; the birds have died out."

Great were the rejoicings at the palace when the King returned in triumph, bringing with him the much-coveted prize, the Golden-breasted Kootoo. The bands played until they almost killed themselves; the cooks waved their ladles and set to work at once on the pie; the huntsmen sang hunting-songs. All was joy and rapture, except in the breast of one man; that man was the Second Musician, or, as we should now call him, the Chief Musician. He felt no thrill of joy at sight of the wondrous bird; on the contrary, he made his will, and prepared to leave the country at once; but when the pie was finished, and he saw its huge dimensions, he was comforted. "No man," he said to himself, "can eat the whole of that pie and live!"

Alas! he was right. The unhappy King fell a victim to his musical ambition before he had half finished his pie, and died in a fit. His subjects ate the remainder of the mighty pasty, with mingled tears and smiles, as a memorial feast; and if the Golden-breasted Kootoo *was* a Shanghai rooster, nobody in the kingdom was ever the wiser for it.

CHAPTER III.

THE raccoon's story was received with general approbation; and the grandmother, in particular, declared she had not passed so pleasant an hour for a very long time. The good woman was gradually becoming accustomed to her strange visitors, and ventured to address them with a little more freedom, though she still trembled and clutched her knitting-needles tighter when she heard the bear's deep tones.

"It is really very good of you all," she said, "to take compassion upon my loneliness. Before I came to this cottage I lived in a large town, where I had many friends, and I find the change very great, and the life here very solitary. Indeed, if it were not for my dear little Toto, I should lead quite the life of a hermit."

"What is a hermit?" asked the bear, who had an inquiring mind, and liked to know the meaning of words.

"It is a crab," said the parrot. "I have often seen them in the West Indies. They get into the shells of other crabs, and drive the owners out. A wretched set!"

"Oh, dear!" cried the grandmother. "That is not at all the kind of hermit I mean. A hermit in this country is a man who lives quite alone, without any companions, in some uninhabited region, such as a wood or a lonely hillside."

"Is it?" exclaimed the bear and the squirrel at the same moment. "Why, then, we know one."

"Certainly," the squirrel went on; "Old Baldhead must be a hermit, of course. He lives alone, and in an uninhabited region; that is, what *you* would call uninhabited, I suppose."

"How very interesting! Where does he live?" asked Toto. "Who is he? How is it that I have never seen him?"

"Oh, he lives quite at the other end of the wood!" replied the squirrel; "some ten miles or more from here. You have never been so far, my dear boy, and Old Baldhead isn't likely to come into our part of the wood. He paid us one visit several years ago, and that was enough for him, eh, Bruin?"

"Humph! I think so!" said Bruin, smiling grimly. "He seemed quite satisfied, I thought."

21

"Tell us about his visit!" cried Toto eagerly. "I have never heard anything about him, and I know it must be funny, or you would not chuckle so, Bruin."

"Well," said the bear, "there isn't much to tell, but you shall hear all I know. *I* call that hermit, if that is his name, a very impudent fellow. Just fancy this, will you? One evening, late in the autumn, about three years ago, I was coming home from a long ramble, very tired and hungry. I had left a particularly nice comb of honey and some other little things in my cave, all ready for supper, for I knew when I started that I should be late, and I was looking forward to a very comfortable evening.

"Well, when I came to the door of my cave, what should I see but an old man with a long gray beard, sitting on the ground eating my honey!" Here the bear looked around with a deeply injured air, and there was a general murmur of sympathy.

"Your course was obvious!" said the raccoon. "Why didn't you eat him, stupid?"

"Hush!" whispered the wood-pigeon softly. "You must not say things like that, Coon! you will frighten the old lady." And indeed, the grandmother seemed much discomposed by the raccoon's suggestion.

"Wouldn't have been polite!" replied Bruin. "My own house, you know, and all that. Besides," he added in an undertone, with an apprehensive glance at the grandmother, "he was old, and probably very—"

"Ahem!" said Toto in a warning voice.

"Oh, certainly not!" said the bear hastily, "not upon any account. I was about to make the same remark myself. A—where was I?"

"The old man was eating your honey," said the woodchuck.

"I only stood up on my hind legs."

"Of course!" replied Bruin. "So, though I would not have hurt him *for the world*" (with another glance towards the grandmother), "I thought there would be no harm in frightening him a little. Accordingly, I first made a great noise among the bushes, snapping the twigs and rustling the leaves at a great rate. He stopped eating, and looked and listened, listened and looked; didn't seem to like it much, I thought. Then, when he was pretty thoroughly roused, I came slowly forward, and planted myself directly in front of the cave."

"Dear me!" cried the grandmother. "How very dreadful! poor old man!"

"Well now, ma'am!" said Bruin appealingly, "he had no right to steal my honey; now had he? And I didn't hurt a hair of his head," he continued. "I only stood up on my hind-legs and waved my fore-paws round and round like a windmill, and roared."

A general burst of merriment greeted this statement, from all except the grandmother, who shuddered in sympathy with the unfortunate hermit.

"Well?" asked Toto, "and what did he do then?"

"Why," said Bruin, "he crouched down in a little heap on the ground, and squeezed himself against the wall of the cave, evidently expecting me to rush upon him and tear him to pieces; I sat down in front of him and looked at him for a few minutes; then, when I thought he had had about enough, I walked past him into the cave, and then he ran away. He has never made me another visit."

"No," said the squirrel; "he went home to his own cave at the other end of the wood, and built a barricade round it, and didn't put his nose out of doors for a week after. I have a cousin who lives in that neighborhood, and he told me about it."

"Have you ever been over there?" asked Toto.

"Yes, indeed!" replied the squirrel, "hundreds of times. I often go over to spend the day with my cousin, and we amuse ourselves by dropping nuts on the hermit's head as he sits in front of his cave. I know few things more amusing," he continued, turning to the grandmother, "than dropping nuts on a bald head. You can make bets as to how high they will go on the rebound. Have you ever tried it, ma'am? sitting in a tree, you know."

"Never!" replied the grandmother with much dignity. "In my youth it was not the custom for gentlewomen to sit in trees for any purpose; and if it had been, I trust I should have had more respect for age and infirmity than to amuse myself in the manner you suggest."

The squirrel was somewhat abashed at this, and scratched his ear to hide his embarrassment.

The pause which ensued gave the raccoon an opportunity for which he had been waiting. He addressed the grandmother in his most honeyed accents:—

"Our ways, dear madam," he said, "are necessarily very different from yours. There must be much in our woodland life that seems rough, and possibly even savage, to a person of refinement and culture like yourself. While we roam about in the untutored forest" ("Hear! hear!" interrupted the squirrel. "'Untutored forest' is good!"), "you remain in the elegant atmosphere of your polished home. While we fare hardly, snatching a precarious and scanty subsistence from roots and herbs, you, lapped in intellectual and highly cultivated leisure, while away the hours by manufacturing gingerbread and—a—jam." The raccoon here waved his tail, and gave Toto a look whose craftiness cannot be described in words.

Toto took the hint. "Dear me!" he cried. "Of course! how stupid of me! Grandmother, is there any gingerbread in the house? My friends have never tasted any, and I should like to give them some of yours."

"Certainly, my dear boy," said the good old lady; "by all means. I have just made some this afternoon. Bring a good plateful, and bring a pot of raspberry jam, too. Perhaps Mr. Coon would like a little of that."

Mr. Coon *did* like a little of that. In fact, Mr. Coon would have liked the whole pot, and would have taken it, too, if it had not been for Toto, who declared that it must be share and share alike. He gave them each a spoon, and let them help themselves in turn, observing the strictest impartiality.

The feast seemed to be highly enjoyed by all.

"Well, Bruin, how do you like jam?" asked Toto.

"Very much, very much indeed!" replied the bear. "Something like honey, isn't it, only entirely different? What kind of creatures make it? Butterflies?"

"Lady makes it herself, stupid!" muttered the woodchuck, who was out of temper, having just tried to get a spoonful out of turn, and failed. "Didn't you hear her say so? Butterflies never make anything except butter."

The little squirrel sat nibbling his gingerbread in a state of great satisfaction. "Who's to tell the story next time?" he asked presently.

"Parrot," answered the raccoon, with his mouth full of jam. "Parrot promised ever so long ago to tell us a story about Africa. Didn't you, Polly?"

The parrot drew herself up with an air of offended dignity. "The gentlemen of my acquaintance, Mr. Coon," she said, "call me Miss Mary. I am 'Polly' to a few intimates only."

"Oh, indeed!" said the raccoon. "I beg your pardon, Miss Mary. No offence, I trust?"

Miss Mary unbent a little, and condescended to explain. "My real name," she said, "is Chamchamchamchamkickeryboo; but, not understanding the subtleties of our African languages, I do not expect you to pronounce that. 'Miss Mary' will do very well; though," she added, "I *have* been called Princess in happier days."

"When was that?" inquired Toto. "Tell us about it, Miss Mary."

"No, no!" interrupted the bear. "No more stories to-night. It is too late. We must be getting home, or the owls will be after us."

"To-morrow, then," cried Toto. "Will you all come to-morrow? Then we will hear the parrot's story."

The animals all promised to come on the morrow, and each in turn took leave of the grandmother, thanking her for the treat they had had. The bear, after making his best bow, led the way towards the forest, followed by the raccoon, the woodchuck, the squirrel, the parrot, and the wood-pigeon. And soon the whole company disappeared among the branches.

CHAPTER IV.

"I was born," said the parrot, "in Africa."

It was a lovely afternoon; and Toto's friends were again assembled around the cottage-door. The parrot, as the story-teller of the day, was perched in great state on the high back of an old-fashioned easy-chair, which Toto had brought out for his grandmother. The old lady sat quietly knitting, with Bruin on one side of her, and Coon on the other; while Toto lay on the grass at her feet, alternately caressing the wood-pigeon and poking the woodchuck to wake him up.

When the parrot said, "I was born in Africa," all the animals looked very wise, but said nothing; so she added, "Of course, you all know where Africa is."

"Of course," said the raccoon hastily; "certainly, I should hope so! We know *where* it is; if you come to that, we know where it is."

"Coon," said Toto, laughing, "what a humbug you are! How is Africa bounded, old fellow? Tell us, if you know so well."

"North by the Gulf States, south by Kalamazoo, east by Mt. Everest, and west by the Straits of Frangipanni," replied the raccoon, without a moment's hesitation.

Miss Mary looked much disgusted. "Africa," she said, "as every person of *education* knows [with a withering glance at the raccoon], is the exact centre of the universe. It is the most beautiful of all lands,—a land of palm-trees and crocodiles, ivory and gold-dust, sunny fountains and—"

"Oh!" cried Toto eagerly, "excuse me for interrupting, Miss Mary; but *are* the sands really golden? 'Where Afric's sunny fountains,' you know, 'roll down their golden sands,'—is that really true?"

"Certainly," replied Miss Mary.

"Dear me, yes. A fountain wouldn't be called a fountain in Africa if it hadn't golden sands. It would be called a cucumber-wood pump," suggested the woodchuck drowsily.

"Toto," said the parrot sharply, "if I am interrupted any more, I shall go home. Will that woodchuck be quiet, or will he not?"

"He will, he will!" cried Toto. "We will all be very quiet, Miss Mary, and not say a word. Pray go on."

Miss Mary smoothed her feathers, which had become quite ruffled, and continued,—

"I was not a common wild parrot,—I should think not, indeed! My mother came of a distinguished family, and was the favorite bird of the great Bhughabhoo, King of Central Africa; and I, as soon as I was fully fledged, became the pet and darling of his only daughter, the Princess Polpetti. Ah! happy, indeed, were the first years of my life! I was the Princess's constant companion. She used to make songs in my honor, and sing them to her royal father while he drank his rum-and-water. They were lovely songs. Would you like to hear one of them?"

All the company declared that it was the one desire of their hearts. So, clearing her throat, and cocking her head on one side, Miss Mary sang:—

"'Chamchamchamchamkickeryboo,

Fairest fowl that ever grew,

Fairest fowl that ever growed,

How you brighten my abode!

How you ornament the view,

Chamchamchamchamkickeryboo!

"'Chamchamchamchamkickeryboo,

You have wit and beauty, too;

You can dance, and you can sing;

You can tie a pudding-string.

Is there aught you *cannot* do,

Chamchamchamchamkickeryboo?'

"That was her opinion of my merits," continued the parrot modestly. "Indeed, it was the general opinion.

"As I was saying, I was the Princess's constant companion. All day I followed her about, sitting on her shoulder, or flying about her head. All night I slept perched on her nose-ring, which she always hung upon a hook when she went to bed.

"Ah! that nose-ring! I wish I had never seen it. It was the cause of all my misfortunes,—of my lovely Princess's death and my own exile. And yet it was a lovely thing in itself.

"I observe, madam," continued the parrot, addressing the grandmother, "that you wear no nose-ring. Such a pity! There is no ornament so becoming. In Africa it is a most important article of dress,—I may say *the* most important. Can I not persuade you to try the effect?"

"Thank you," replied the grandmother, smiling. "I fear I am too old, Miss Mary, even if it were the custom in this country to wear nose-rings, which I believe it is not. But how was the Princess's nose-ring the cause of your misfortunes? Pray tell us."

The parrot looked sadly at the grandmother's nose, and shook her head. "Such a pity!" she repeated. "It would be so becoming! You would never regret it. However," she added, "you shall hear the rest of my sad story.

"The Princess's nose-ring was, as you may infer from the fact of my being able to swing in it, a very large one. She was a connoisseur in nose-rings, and had a large collection of them, of which collection this was the gem. It was of beaten gold, incrusted with precious stones. No other nose in the kingdom could have sustained such a weight; but hers—ah, hers was a nose in a thousand."

"Pardon me!" said the raccoon softly, "do I understand that a long nose is considered a beauty in Africa?"

"It is, indeed," replied the parrot. "It is, indeed. You would be much admired in Africa, Mr. Coon."

The raccoon looked sidewise at his sharp-pointed nose, and stroked it complacently. "Ah!" he observed, "I agree with you, Miss Mary, as to Africa being the centre of the earth. Pray go on."

"I need hardly say," continued the parrot, "that the jewelled nose-ring was the envy of all the other princesses for miles around. Foremost among the envious ones was the Princess Panka, the daughter of a neighboring king. She never could have worn the nose-ring; her nose was less than half an inch long, and she was altogether hideous; but she wanted it, and she made up her mind to get it by foul means, if fair ones would not do. Accordingly she bribed the Princess's bogghun."

"The Princess's *what?*" asked the bear.

"Bogghun," repeated the parrot testily. "The Princess's bogghun! Don't tell me you don't know what a bogghun is!"

"Well, I don't," replied sturdy Bruin; "and what's more, I don't believe any one else does!"

The parrot looked around, but as no one seemed inclined to give any information respecting bogghuns, she continued, "The bogghun is a kind of lizard, found only on the island of Bogghun-Chunka. It is about five feet long, of a brilliant green color. It invariably holds the end of its tail in its mouth, and moves by rolling, while in this position, like a child's hoop. In fact, it is used as a hoop by African children; hence the term 'bogghun.' It feeds on the chunka, a triangular yellow beetle found in the same locality; hence the name of the island, Bogghun-Chunka.

"She caressed the bogghun."

"The bogghun is a treacherous animal, as I have found to my cost. The one belonging to my mistress was a very beautiful creature, and much beloved by her, yet he betrayed her in the basest manner, as you shall hear.

"The Princess Panka, finding that the bogghun was very fond of molasses candy, bribed him by the offer of three pounds of that condiment to deliver the Princess into her hands. The plot was arranged, and the day set. On that day, as usual, the bogghun rolled up to the door after dinner, and the Princess, taking me on her shoulder, went out for her usual afternoon play. She caressed the bogghun,—ah! faithless wretch! how could he bear the touch of that gentle hand?—and then struck him lightly with her silver hoop-stick; he rolled swiftly away, and we followed, Polpetti bounding as lightly as a deer, while I sat upon her shoulder, undisturbed by the rapid motion.

"Away rolled the bogghun, away and away, over the meadows and into the forest; away and away bounded the Princess in pursuit. The golden nose-ring flashed and glittered in the sunlight; the golden bangles on her wrists and ankles tinkled and rang their tiny bells as she went. Faster and faster! faster and faster! The monkeys, swinging by their tails from the branches, chattered with astonishment at us; the wild parrots screamed at us; all the birds sang and chirped and twittered,—

'Come! come! tweedle-dee-dum!

See! see! tweedle-de-dee!

Hi! hi! kikeriki!

They have no wings, and yet they fly.'

And truly we did seem to fly, so swift was our motion. At length I became alarmed, and begged the Princess to turn back. She had never before gone so far in the forest unattended, I told her; and there was no knowing what dangers might lurk in its leafy depths. But, alas! she was too much excited to listen to my remonstrances. On and on rolled the treacherous bogghun, and on and on she bounded in pursuit.

"Suddenly, as we went skimming across an open glade, a sharp twang was heard: I saw a white flash in the air; and the next moment I was hurled violently to the ground. Recovering myself in an instant, I saw my lovely Princess stretched lifeless on the ground, with an arrow quivering in her heart!

"At the same moment the bogghun stopped; and out from the surrounding coppice rushed the Princess Panka and her attendants.

"'Where is my molasses candy?' asked the bogghun. Three of the attendants presented him with three one-pound packages; and thus in a moment I understood the whole villanous plot. The Princess Panka rushed to where Polpetti lay, and snatched the golden nose-ring from her lovely nose. Fastening it in her own hideous snub, she sprang to her feet with a shrill yell of triumph. 'At last!' she cried,—'at last I have it!'

"'Hideous witch!' I exclaimed. 'You have no nose to wear it in! You are uglier than the blue-faced monkey, or the toad with three tails. The very sight of you makes the leaves drop off the trees with horror. You odious, squint-eyed—'

"'Catch that parrot!' shrieked the enraged Panka. 'Wring that parrot's neck! Pull his feathers out! Let me get at him!'

30

"I rose in the air, and flying round her head, continued—'Snub-nosed, monkey-faced, bald-headed [this adjective was not exactly correct, but I was too angry to choose my words], hump-backed *Ant-eater*!!!' and with the last word, the most opprobrious epithet that can be applied to an African, I gave the creature a peck in the face that sent her tumbling over backwards, and flew off among the trees. A storm of arrows followed me, but I escaped unhurt, and flying rapidly, was soon far away from the spot."

"'Hideous witch!' I exclaimed."

Here the parrot paused to take breath, having become quite excited in telling her story.

"Ahem!" said the woodchuck. "May I be permitted to ask a question, Miss Mary?"

"Certainly," replied the parrot graciously. "What is it, Woodchuck?"

"Did I understand," said the woodchuck cautiously, "that the bogghun *never* takes his tail out of his mouth?"

"Never!" replied the parrot. "Never, upon any occasion!"

"Then how," asked Chucky, "did he eat the molasses candy?"

"Woodchuck," said the parrot, with great severity, "the question does credit neither to your head nor to your heart. I decline to answer it!"

The woodchuck looked sulky, and scratched his nose expressively. The raccoon, who had been on the point of asking the same question himself, frowned at him, and said he was ashamed of him. "Pray continue your story, Miss Mary!" said he. "I assure you we are all, with perhaps *one* exception [the woodchuck sniffed audibly], quite faint with excitement and suspense. What became of you after the Princess's death?"

"I remained in the forest," said the parrot. "I could not go back to the village without the Princess; the King would have put me to death if I had made my appearance.

"For some time I lived alone, associating as little as possible with the uneducated birds of the forest. At length, finding my life very solitary, I accepted the claw and heart of a rich and respectable green parrot, who offered me a good home and the devotion of a life-time. With him I passed several quiet and happy years; but finally we were both surprised and captured by a band of American sailors, who had penetrated to this distance in the forest in search of ivory. They treated us kindly, and carried us miles and miles till we came to a river, where other sailors were waiting with a boat. In this we embarked, and after rowing for several days, came to the mouth of the river, near which their ship was waiting for them.

"In the confusion of boarding, my husband managed to make his escape. He flew back to the shore, calling to me to follow him; but, alas! I was too closely guarded, and I never saw him again. He was a very worthy parrot, and a kind husband, though sometimes greedy in the matter of snails."

The parrot sighed, meditated for a few moments, with her head on one side, on the virtues of her departed lord, and then continued,—

"My life on board ship was a very pleasant one. Petted and caressed by the sailors, I soon lost my shyness, and became once more accustomed to the society of men. I learned English quickly, and could soon whistle 'Yankee Doodle' and 'Three Cheers for the Red, White, and Blue.' One phrase I objected very much to repeating, 'Polly wants a cracker.' I disliked crackers extremely, and could not endure the name of Polly; but for some time I could not get anything to eat without making this stupid remark.

"One day I received a shock which nearly caused me to faint. I was sitting on the taffrail, watching two of my particular friends, Joe Brown and Simeon Plunkett, who were splicing ropes. They always spliced better, I noticed, when my eye was on them. They were talking about some adventure in the forest, and suddenly I caught the words, 'golden nose-ring.' I had been half dozing; but this roused me at once, and I began to listen with all my ears."

"How many ears has she?" growled the woodchuck, in a low tone.

"Twenty-five," replied the raccoon, in the same tone. "They are invisible to idiots, which is probably the reason why you have never noticed them."

"'How did you get that nose-ring?' asked Joe Brown. 'You have begun to tell me once or twice, and something has always stopped you. Were there many of them lying around? I shouldn't mind having that myself.'

"Judge of my feelings when Simeon Plunkett, before replying, pulled out from the breast of his flannel shirt a huge golden ring, set with jewels,—*the* identical golden nose-ring which had caused the death of my lovely Princess. I shuddered, and came very near falling from the taffrail; but, composing myself, I listened eagerly, and heard Simeon tell the other how, as he and his mates were returning to their boat (he had been with a second exploring party sent out from the ship), they found a well, and stopped to fish in it."

"To fish in a well?" interrupted Bruin. "What did they do that for?"

"To see what they could catch," replied the parrot. "What do people fish for in this country?

"The first thing they caught was the body of a young woman, with this golden ring in her nose. Her feet were up, and her head was down; and altogether, Simeon said, it was very evident that, in stooping over either to drink or to admire her beauty in the well, the weight of the ring had overbalanced her, and caused her to fall in.

"When I heard this news I flapped my wings and crowed, to the great astonishment of the two sailors. My enemy was dead, and Polpetti avenged. My joy was great, and I wanted to thank Simeon Plunkett for being the bearer of such good news; so I perched on his knee, and sang him the sweetest song I knew,—a song which had often brought tears to the eyes of my lost husband. But he only said, 'Princess [they all called me Princess, I should observe], if any other bird made such a row as that, I'd wring its neck.' The Americans, I find, have absolutely *no* ear for music.

"We reached America after a pleasant and prosperous voyage.

"But he only said, 'Princess, if any other bird made such a row as that, I'd wring its neck.'"

"After that my adventures may be told in a few words. Joe Brown presented me, as a great treasure, to the captain's wife, Mrs. Jeremy Jibb; but I found her a most unpleasant person to live with. She kept me in a cage,—a tin cage,—me, the favorite companion of the Princess Royal of Central Africa! She fed me on crackers, called me Polly all the time, and treated me in a most degrading manner generally. If I had been a canary-bird, her manner could not have been more insufferably patronizing. After enduring this life for several weeks, I managed to make my escape one day while Mrs. Jibb was cleaning my cage.

After a long flight, I reached this forest, in whose pleasant retirement I have remained ever since. Here I find society and snails, both of excellent quality; and, with these, what more does one require? And here I hope to pass the remainder of my days."

The parrot's story, with the various pauses and interruptions, had occupied a good deal of time; and when it was finished the party broke up, promising to reassemble on the following day. Before they separated, Toto asked, as usual, who was to tell the next story.

"Tell it yourself, Toto," said the wood-pigeon; and all the rest chimed in, "Yes, Toto shall tell the next himself." So it was settled; and they all shook paws, and departed.

CHAPTER V.

THE next day it rained, so the party of friends did not assemble as usual. The bear stayed in his cave, sucking his paw, and listening to the chatter of the squirrel, who came to spend the day with him. The raccoon, after one look at the weather, curled himself up in his tree-house and went to sleep. As for the woodchuck, he never woke up at all, for nobody came to wake him, and he could not do it for himself.

Poor Toto was very disconsolate. He never stayed indoors for an ordinary rain, but this was a perfect deluge; so he stood by the window and said, "Oh, dear! oh, *dear*!! oh, DEAR!!!" as if he did not know how to say anything else.

His good grandmother bore this quietly for some time; but at length she said, "Toto, do you know what happened to the boy who said 'Oh, dear!' too many times?"

"No!" said Toto, brightening up at the prospect of a story. "What did happen to him? Tell me, Granny, please!"

"Come and hold this skein of yarn for me, then," replied the grandmother, "and I will tell you as I wind it.

"Once upon a time there was a boy—"

"What was his name?" interrupted Toto.

"Chimborazo," replied the grandmother. "I should have told you his real name in a moment, if you had not interrupted me, but now I shall call him Chimborazo, and that will be something for you to remember."

Toto blushed and hung his head.

"This boy," continued the grandmother, "invariably put the wrong foot out of bed first when he got up in the morning, and consequently he was always unhappy."

"May I speak?" murmured Toto softly.

"Yes, you may speak," said the old lady. "What is it?"

"Please, grandmother," said Toto, "which *is* the wrong foot?"

"Don't you know which your right foot is?" asked the grandmother.

"Why, yes, of course," replied Toto.

"And do you know the difference between right and wrong?"

"Why, yes, of course," said Toto.

"Then," said the grandmother, "you know which the wrong foot is.

"As I was saying, Chimborazo was a very unhappy boy. He pouted, and he sulked, and he said, 'Oh, dear! oh, dear! oh, dear! oh, dear!' He said it till everybody was tired of hearing it.

"'Chimborazo,' his mother would say, 'please don't say, "Oh, dear!" any more. It is very annoying. Say something else.'

"'Oh, dear!' the boy would answer, 'I can't! I don't know anything else to say. Oh, dear! oh, *dear*! oh, DEAR!!!'

"So one day his mother could not bear it any longer, and she sent for his fairy godmother, and told her all about it.

"'Humph!' said the fairy godmother. 'I will see to it. Send the boy to me!'

"So Chimborazo was sent for, and came, hanging his head as usual. When he saw his fairy godmother, he said, 'Oh, dear!' for he was rather afraid of her.

"'"Oh, dear!" it is!' said the godmother sharply; and she put on her spectacles and looked at him. 'Do you know what a bell-punch is?'

"'Oh, dear!' said Chimborazo. 'No, ma'am, I don't!'

"'Well,' said the godmother, 'I am going to give you one.'

"'Oh, dear!' said Chimborazo, 'I don't want one.'

"'Probably not,' replied she, 'but that doesn't make much difference. You have it now, in your jacket pocket.'

"Chimborazo felt in his pocket, and took out a queer-looking instrument of shining metal. 'Oh, dear!' he said.

""Oh, dear!" it is!' said the fairy godmother. 'Now,' she continued, 'listen to me, Chimborazo! I am going to put you on an allowance of "Oh, dears." This is a self-acting bell-punch, and it will ring whenever you say "Oh, dear!" How many times do you generally say it in the course of the day?'

"'Oh, dear!' said Chimborazo, 'I don't know. Oh, *dear*!'

"'*Ting! ting!*' the bell-punch rang twice sharply; and looking at it in dismay, he saw two little round holes punched in a long slip of pasteboard which was fastened to the instrument.

"'Exactly!' said the fairy. 'That is the way it works, and a very pretty way, too. Now, my boy, I am going to make you a very liberal allowance. You may say "Oh, dear!" forty-five times a day. There's liberality for you!'

"'Oh, dear!' cried Chimborazo, 'I—'

"'*Ting!*' said the bell-punch.

"'You see!' observed the fairy. 'Nothing could be prettier. You have now had three of this day's allowance. It is still some hours before noon, so I advise you to be careful. If you exceed the allowance—' Here she paused, and glowered through her spectacles in a very dreadful manner.

"'Oh, dear!' cried Chimborazo. 'What will happen then?'

"'You will see!' said the fairy godmother, with a nod. '*Something* will happen, you may be very sure of that. Good-by. Remember, only forty-five!' And away she flew out of the window.

"'Oh, dear!' cried Chimborazo, bursting into tears. 'I don't want it! I won't have it! Oh, *dear*! oh, dear! oh, dear! oh, dear! oh, DEAR!!!'

"Good-by. Remember, only forty-five!"

"'Ting! ting! ting-ting-ting-*ting*!' said the bell-punch; and now there were ten round holes in the strip of pasteboard. Chimborazo was now really frightened. He was silent for some time; and when his mother called him to his lessons he tried very hard not to say the dangerous words. But the habit was so strong that he said them unconsciously. By dinner-time there were twenty-five holes in the cardboard strip; by tea-time there were forty! Poor Chimborazo! he was afraid to open his lips, for whenever he did the words would slip out in spite of him.

"'Well, Chimbo,' said his father after tea, 'I hear you have had a visit from your fairy godmother. What did she say to you, eh?'

"'Oh, dear!' said Chimborazo, 'she said—oh, dear! I've said it again!'

"'She said, "Oh, dear! I've said it again!"' repeated his father. 'What do you mean by that?'

"'Oh, dear! I didn't mean that,' cried Chimborazo hastily; and again the inexorable bell rang, and he knew that another hole was punched in the fatal cardboard. He pressed his lips firmly together, and did not open them again except to say 'Good-night,' until he was safe in his own room. Then he hastily drew the hated bell-punch from his pocket, and counted the holes in the strip of cardboard; there were forty-three! 'Oh, *dear*!' cried the boy, forgetting himself again in his alarm, 'only two more! Oh, *dear*! oh, DEAR! I've done it again! oh—' 'Ting! TING!' went the bell-punch; and the cardboard was punched to the end. 'Oh, dear!' cried Chimborazo, now beside himself with terror. 'Oh, dear! oh, dear! oh, dear! oh, *dear*!! what will become of me?'

"A strange whirring noise was heard, then a loud clang; and the next moment the bell-punch, as if it were alive, flew out of his hand, out of the window, and was gone!

"Chimborazo stood breathless with terror for a few minutes, momentarily expecting that the roof would fall in on his head, or the floor blow up under his feet, or some appalling catastrophe of some kind follow; but nothing followed. Everything was quiet, and there seemed to be nothing to do but go to bed; so to bed he went, and slept, only to dream that he was shot through the head with a bell-punch, and died saying, 'Oh, dear!'

"The next morning, when Chimborazo came downstairs, his father said, 'My boy, I am going to drive over to your grandfather's farm this morning; would you like to go with me?'

"A drive to the farm was one of the greatest pleasures Chimborazo had, so he answered promptly, 'Oh, *dear*!'

"'Oh, very well!' said his father, looking much surprised. 'You need not go, my son, if you do not want to. I will take Robert instead.'

"Poor Chimborazo! He had opened his lips to say, 'Thank you, papa. I should like to go *very* much!' and, instead of these words, out had popped, in his most doleful tone, the now hated 'Oh, dear!' He sat amazed; but was roused by his mother's calling him to breakfast.

"'Come, Chimbo,' she said. 'Here are sausages and scrambled eggs; and you are very fond of both of them. Which will you have?'

"Chimborazo hastened to say, 'Sausages, please, mamma,'—that is, he hastened to *try* to say it; but all his mother heard was, 'Oh, *dear*!'

"His father looked much displeased. 'Give the boy some bread and water, wife,' he said sternly. 'If he cannot answer properly, he must be taught. I have had enough of this "Oh, dear!" business.'

"Poor Chimborazo! He saw plainly enough now what his punishment was to be; and the thought of it made him tremble. He tried to ask for some more bread, but only brought out his 'Oh, *dear*!' in such a lamentable tone that his father ordered him to leave the room. He went out into the garden, and there he met John the gardener, carrying a basket of rosy apples. Oh! how good they looked!

"'I am bringing some of the finest apples up to the house, little master,' said John. 'Will you have one to put in your pocket?'

"'Oh, *dear*!' was all the poor boy could say, though he wanted an apple, oh, so much! And when John heard that he put the apple back in his basket, muttering something about ungrateful monkeys.

"Poor Chimborazo! I will not give the whole history of that miserable day,—a miserable day it was from beginning to end. He fared no better at dinner than at breakfast; for at the second 'Oh, dear!' his father sent him up to his room, 'to stay there until he knew how to take what was given him, and be thankful for it.' He knew well enough by this time; but he could not tell his father so. He went to his room, and sat looking out of the window, a hungry and miserable boy.

"In the afternoon his cousin Will came up to see him. 'Why, Chimbo!' he cried. 'Why do you sit moping here in the house, when all the boys are out? Come and play marbles with me on the piazza. Ned and Harry are out there waiting for you. Come on!'

"'Oh, dear!' said Chimborazo.

"'What's the matter?' asked Will. 'Haven't you any marbles? Never mind. I'll give you half of mine, if you like. Come!'

"'Oh, DEAR!' said Chimborazo.

"'Well,' said Will, 'if that's all you have to say when I offer you marbles, I'll keep them myself. I suppose you expected me to give you all of them, did you? I never saw such a fellow!' and off he went in a huff.

"'Well, Chimborazo,' said the fairy godmother, 'what do you think of "Oh, dear!" now?'

"Touching his lips with her wand."

"Chimborazo looked at her beseechingly, but said nothing.

"'Finding that forty-five times was not enough for you yesterday, I thought I would let you have all you wanted to-day, you see,' said the fairy wickedly.

"The boy still looked imploringly at her, but did not open his lips.

"'Well, well,' she said at last, touching his lips with her wand, 'I think that is enough in the way of punishment, though I am sorry you broke the bell-punch. Good-by! I don't believe you will say "Oh, dear!" any more.'

"And he didn't."

CHAPTER VI.

THE rain continued for several days; and though Toto, mindful of the sad story of Chimborazo, tried hard not to say "Oh, dear!" still he found the time hang very heavy on his hands. On the fourth day, however, the clouds broke away, and the sun came out bright and beautiful. Toto snatched up his cap, kissed his grandmother, and flew off to the forest. Oh, how glad he was to be out of doors again, and how glad everything seemed to be to see him! All the trees shook down pearls and diamonds on him (very wet ones they were, but he did not mind that), the birds sang to him, the flowers nodded to him, the sunbeams twinkled at him; everything seemed to say, "How are you, Toto? Hasn't it been a lovely rain, and aren't you glad it is over?"

He went straight to the forest pool, hoping to find some of his companions there. Sure enough, there was the raccoon, sitting by the edge of the pool, making his toilet, and stopping every now and then to gaze admiringly at himself in the clear mirror.

"Good-morning, Coon!" said Toto; "admiring your beauty as usual, eh?"

"Well, Toto," replied the raccoon complacently, "my view of the matter is this: what is the use of having beauty if you don't admire it? That is what it's for, I suppose."

"I suppose so," assented Toto.

"And you can't expect other people to admire you if you don't admire yourself!" added the raccoon impressively. "Remember that! How's your grandmother?"

"She's very well," replied Toto, "and she hopes to see you all this afternoon. She has made a new kind of gingerbread, and she wants you to try it. I have tried it, and it is very good indeed."

"Your grandmother," said the raccoon, "is in many respects the most delightful person I have ever met. I, for one, will come with pleasure. I can't tell about the rest; haven't seen them for a day or two. Suppose we go and hunt them up."

"With all my heart!" said Toto.

They had not gone far before they met the wood-pigeon flying along with a bunch of berries in her bill.

"Where are you going, Pigeon Pretty?" inquired Toto; "and who is to have those nice berries? I am sure they are not for yourself; I believe you never get anything for yourself, you are so busy helping others."

"These berries are for poor Chucky," replied the wood-pigeon. "Ah, Coon," she added reproachfully, "how could you hurt the poor fellow so? He is really ill this morning in consequence."

"What have you been doing to Chucky, you naughty Coon?" asked Toto. "Biting his nose off?"

"Oh, no!" said the raccoon, looking rather guilty, in spite of his assurance. "Dear me, no! I didn't bite it *off*. Certainly not! I—I just bit it a little, don't you know! it was raining, and I hadn't anything else to do; and he was *so* sound asleep, it was a great temptation. But I won't do it again, Pigeon Pretty," he added cheerfully, "I won't really. Take him the berries, with my love, and say I hope they will do him good!" and with a crafty wink, Master Coon trotted on with Toto, while Pigeon Pretty flew off in the opposite direction.

They soon arrived at the mouth of the bear's cave, and looking in, saw the worthy Bruin quietly playing backgammon with his devoted friend Cracker. The latter was chattering as usual. "And so *I* said to him," he was saying as Toto and Coon approached, "'*I* think it is a mean trick, and I'll have nothing to do with it. And what is more, I'll put a stop to it if I can!' So he said he'd like to see me do it, and flounced off into the water."

"Humph!" said Bruin, "I never did think much of that muskrat."

"What's all this?" asked the raccoon, walking in. "Anything the matter, Cracker?"

"Bruin playing backgammon with his friend Cracker."

"Good-morning, Coon!" said Bruin. "Morning, Toto! Sit down, both of you. Cracker was just telling me—"

"It is that muskrat that lives in the pool, you know, Coon!" broke in the squirrel excitedly. "He wants to marry the Widow Bullfrog's daughter, and she won't have him, because she's engaged to young Mud Turtle. So now the muskrat has contrived a plan for carrying her off to-night whether she will or no; and if you will believe it, he came to *me* and asked me to help him,—me, the head squirrel of the whole forest!" and little Cracker whisked his tail about fiercely, and looked as if he could devour a whole army of muskrats.

"Don't frighten us, Cracker!" said the raccoon, with a look of mock terror. "I shall faint if you look so ferocious. I shall, indeed! Hold me, Toto!"

"Now, Coon, you know I won't have Cracker teased!" growled the bear. "He's a good little fellow, and if he wants to help the Widow Bullfrog out of this scrape, he shall. I believe she is a very respectable person. Now, I don't know whether I can do anything about it myself. I'm rather large, you see, and it won't do for me to go paddling about in the pool and getting the water all muddy."

"Certainly not!" said the squirrel, "you dear old monster. I should as soon think of asking the mountain to come and hunt mosquitoes. But Coon, now—"

"Oh, I'm ready!" exclaimed the raccoon. "Delighted, I'm sure, to do anything I can. What shall I do to the muskrat? Eat him?"

"I suppose that would be the easiest thing to do," said the bear. "What do you say, Cracker?"

"He is very hard to catch," replied the squirrel. "In fact, you *cannot* catch a muskrat unless you put tar on his nose."

"That is true," said the raccoon. "I had forgotten that, and I haven't any tar just now. Would pitch or turpentine do as well, do you think? They all begin with 'A', you know."

"I'm afraid not!" said the squirrel. "'Tar to catch a Tartar,' as the old saying goes; and the muskrat is certainly a Tartar."

"Look here!" said Toto, "I think we have some tar at home, in the shed. I am quite sure there is some."

"Really?" said the squirrel, brightening up. "Good boy, Toto! Tell me where I can find it, and I'll go and get it."

"No!" said Toto. "It's in a bucket, and you couldn't carry it, Cracker! I'll go and fetch it, while you and Coon are arranging your plan of action."

So away ran Toto, and the squirrel and the raccoon sat down to consult.

"The first thing to do," said Coon, "is to get the muskrat out of his hole. Now, my advice is this: do you go to Mrs. Bullfrog, and borrow an old overcoat of her husband's."

"Husband's dead," said the bear.

"That's no reason why his overcoat should be dead, stupid!" replied the raccoon. "It isn't likely that he was buried in his overcoat, and it isn't likely that she has cut it up for a riding-habit. Borrow the overcoat," he continued, turning to the squirrel again, "and put it on. Old Bullfrog was a very big fellow, and I think you can get it on. Then you can sit on a stone and whistle like a frog."

"I can't sit down in a frog's overcoat!" objected the squirrel. "I know I can't. It's not the right shape, and I don't sit down in that way. And I can't whistle like a frog either."

"Dear me!" said the raccoon peevishly. "What *can* you do? I am sure *I* could sit down in any coat I could wear at all. Well, then," he added after a pause, "you can *stand* on a stone, and *look* like a frog. I suppose you can do that?"

"I suppose so," said Cracker, dubiously.

"And Toto," continued the raccoon, "can hide himself in the reeds on one side of you, and I on the other. Toto whistles beautifully, and he can imitate Miss Bullfrog's voice to perfection. The muskrat will be sure to come up when he hears it, and the moment he pops his head out of the water, you can drop some tar on his nose, and *then—*"

"Then what?" asked the squirrel anxiously.

"I will attend to the rest of it," said Coon, with a wink. "See that I have cards to the Mud Turtle's wedding, will you? Here comes Toto," he added, "with tar enough to catch fifty muskrats. Off with you, Cracker, and ask the Widow Frog for the overcoat."

The squirrel disappeared among the bushes, and at the same time Toto came running up with the tar-bucket.

"Well," he said breathlessly, "is it all arranged? Oh! I ran all the way, and I am *so* tired!" and he dropped down on a mossy seat, and fanned himself with his cap.

Bruin brought a piece of honeycomb to refresh him, and Coon told him the proposed plan, which delighted the boy greatly.

"And I am to do the whistling?" he exclaimed. "I must practise a bit, for I have not done any frog-whistling for some time." And with that he began to whistle in such a wonderfully frog-like way, that Bruin almost thought he must have swallowed a frog.

"How do you do that, Toto?" he asked. "I wish I could learn. You just purse your mouth up so, eh? Ugh! wah! woonk!" And the bear gave a series of most surprising grunts and growls, accompanied with such singular grimaces that both Toto and the raccoon rolled over on the ground in convulsions of laughter.

"My dear Bruin," cried Toto, as soon as he could regain a little composure, "I don't think—ha! ha! ha!—I really do *not* think you will ever be mistaken for a frog."

"Ho! ho! ho!" cried the raccoon, bursting into another fit of laughter as he looked towards the mouth of the cave. "Look at Cracker. Oh, my eye! *will* you look at Cracker? Oh, dear me! I shall certainly die if I laugh any more. Ho! ho!"

Bruin and Toto turned, and saw the squirrel hobbling in, dressed in a green frog-skin, and looking—well, did you ever see a squirrel in a frog-skin? No? Then you never saw the funniest thing in the world.

Poor Cracker, however, seemed to see no fun in it at all. "It's all very well for you fellows to laugh," he said ruefully. "I wonder how you would like to be pinched up in an abominable, ill-fitting thing like this? Ugh! I wouldn't be a frog for all the beechnuts in the world. Come on!" he added sharply. "Let us get the matter over, and have done with it. I can't stand this long."

Accordingly the three started off, leaving Bruin shaking his head and chuckling at the mouth of the cave.

Arrived at the pool, they stationed themselves as had been previously arranged: the squirrel on a large stone at the very edge of the pool, with the tar-bucket beside him; the raccoon crouching among the tall reeds on one side of the stone, while Toto lay closely hidden on the other, behind a clump of tall ferns.

When all was ready, Toto began to whistle. At first he whistled very softly, but gradually the notes swelled, growing clearer and shriller, till they seemed to fill the air.

Presently a ripple was seen in the clear water, and the sharp black nose of a muskrat appeared above the surface. "Lovely creature!" exclaimed the muskrat. "Adored Miss Bullfrog, is it possible that you have changed your mind, and decided to listen to my suit?"

"'Oh, rapture!' cried the muskrat."

"I have," said the squirrel softly.

"Oh, rapture!" cried the muskrat. "Come, then, at once with me! Let us fly, or rather swim, before your tyrannical parent discovers us! Leap down, my lovely one, with your accustomed grace and agility, into the arms of your faithful, your adoring muskrat! Come!"

"You must come a little nearer," whispered the squirrel coyly. "I want to be sure that it is *really* you; such a sudden step, you know! Please put your whole head out, my love, that I may be *quite* sure of you!"

The eager muskrat thrust his head out of the water; and plump! the squirrel dropped the tar on the end of his nose.

The muskrat gave a wild shriek, and plunging his nose among the rushes on the bank, tried to rub off the tar. But, alas! the tar stuck to the rushes, and his nose stuck to the tar, and there he was!

At that instant the raccoon leaped from his hiding-place.

Toto, still concealed behind the clump of ferns, heard the noise of a violent struggle; then came several short squeaks; then a crunching noise; and then silence. Coming out from his hiding-place, he saw the raccoon sitting quietly on a stone, licking his chops, and smoothing his ruffled fur.

He smiled sweetly at Toto, and said, "It's all right, my boy! you whistled beautifully; couldn't have done it better myself!" (N. B. Coon's whistling powers were nearly equal to those of the bear.)

"But where is the muskrat?" asked Toto, bewildered. "What have you done with him?"

"Eaten him, my dear!" replied Coon, benignly. "It is always the best plan in any case of this sort; saves trouble, you see, and prevents any further inquiry in the matter; besides, I was always taught in my youth never to waste anything. The flavor was not all I could have wished," he added, "and there was more or less stringiness; but what will not one do in the cause of friendship! Don't mention it, Cracker, my boy! I am sure you would have done as much for me. And now let us help you off with the overcoat of the late lamented Bullfrog; for to speak in perfect frankness, Cracker, it is *not* what one would call becoming to your style of beauty."

CHAPTER VII.

ON account of the woodchuck's illness, and at the special request of Pigeon Pretty, the story-telling was postponed for a day or two. Very soon, however, Chucky recovered sufficiently to ride as far as the cottage on Bruin's back; and on a fine afternoon the friends were all once more assembled, and waiting for Toto's story.

"I don't know any long stories," said Toto, "at least not well enough to tell them; so I will tell two short ones instead. Will that do?"

"Just as well," said the raccoon. "Five minutes for refreshments between the two, did you say? My view precisely."

Toto smiled, and began the story of

THE TRAVELLER, THE COOK, AND THE LITTLE OLD MAN.

Once upon a time there was a little old man who lived in a well. He was a very small little old man, and the well was very deep; and the only reason why he lived there was because he could not get out. Indeed, what better reason could he have?

He had long white hair, and a long red nose, and a long green coat; and this was all he had in the world, except a three-legged stool, a large iron kettle, and a cook. There was not room in the well for the cook; so she lived on the ground above, and cooked the little old man's dinner and supper in the iron kettle, and lowered them down to him in the bucket; and the little old man sat on the three-legged stool, and ate whatever the cook sent down to him, with a cheerful heart, if it was good; and so things went on very pleasantly.

"The old man thought it was raining."

But one day it happened that the cook could not find anything for the old man's dinner. She looked high, and she looked low, but nothing could she find; so she was very unhappy; for she knew her master would be miserable if he had no dinner. She sat down by the well, and wept bitterly; and her tears fell into the well so fast that the little old man thought it was raining, and put up a red cotton umbrella, which he borrowed for the occasion. You may wonder where he borrowed it; but I cannot tell you, because I do not know.

Now, at that moment a traveller happened to pass by, and when he saw the cook sitting by the well and weeping, he stopped, and asked her what was the matter. So the cook told him that she was weeping because she could not find anything to cook for her master's dinner.

"And who is your master?" asked the traveller.

"He is a little old man," replied the cook; "and he lives down in this well."

"Why does he live there?" inquired the traveller.

"I do not know," answered the cook; "I never asked him."

"He must be a singular person," said the traveller. "I should like to see him. What does he look like?"

But this the cook could not tell him; for she had never seen the little old man, having come to work for him after he had gone down to live in the well.

"Does he like to receive visitors?" asked the traveller.

"Don't know," said the cook. "He has never had any to receive since I have been here."

"Humph!" said the other. "I think I will go down and pay my respects to him. Will you let me down in the bucket?"

"But suppose he should mistake you for his dinner, and eat you up?" the cook suggested.

"Pooh!" he replied. "No fear of that; I can take care of myself. And as for his dinner," he added, "get him some radishes. There are plenty about here. I had nothing but radishes for my dinner, and very good they were, though rather biting. Let down the bucket, please! I am all right."

"What are radishes?" the cook called after him as he went down.

"Long red things, stupid! with green leaves to them!" he shouted; and then, in a moment, he found himself at the bottom of the well.

The little old man was delighted to see him, and told him that he had lived down there forty years, and had never had a visitor before in all that time.

"Why do you live down here?" inquired the traveller.

"Because I cannot get out," replied the little old man.

"But how did you get down here in the first place?"

"Really," he said, "it is so long ago that I hardly remember. My impression is, however, that I came down in the bucket."

"Then why, in the name of common-sense," said the traveller, "don't you go *up* in the bucket?"

The little old man sprang up from the three-legged stool, and flung his arms around the traveller's neck. "My *dear* friend!" he cried rapturously. "My precious benefactor! Thank you a thousand times for those words! I assure you I never thought of it before! I will go up at once. You will excuse me?"

"Certainly," said the traveller. "Go up first, and I will follow you."

The little old man got into the bucket, and was drawn up to the top of the well. But, alas! when the cook saw his long red nose and his long green coat, she said to herself, "This must be a radish! How lucky I am!" and seizing the poor little old man, she popped him into the kettle without more ado. Then she let the bucket down for the traveller, calling to him to make haste, as she wanted to send down her master's dinner.

"'Tis an ill wind that blows nobody any good!"

Up came the traveller, and looking around, asked where her master was.

"Where should he be," said the cook, "but at the bottom of the well, where you left him?"

"What do you mean?" exclaimed the traveller. "He has just come up in the bucket!"

"*Oh!*" cried the cook. "Oh! *oh!!* o-o-o-H!!! was that my master? Why, I thought he was a radish, and I have boiled him for his own dinner!"

"I hope he will have a good appetite!" said the traveller.

The cook was a good woman, and her grief was so excessive that she fell into the kettle and was boiled too.

Then the traveller, who had formerly been an ogre by profession, said, "'Tis an ill wind that blows nobody any good! My dinner was very insufficient;" and he ate both the little old man and the cook, and proceeded on his journey with a cheerful heart.

"The traveller was a sensible man," said Bruin. "Did you make up that story, Toto?"

"Yes," replied Toto. "I made it up the other day,—one of those rainy days. I found a forked radish in the bunch we had for tea, and it had a kind of nose, and looked just like a funny little red man. So I thought that if there was a radish that looked like a man, there might be a man that looked like a radish, you see. And now—"

"Ahem!" said the raccoon softly. "*Did* you say five minutes for refreshments, Toto, or did I misunderstand you?" and he winked at the company in a very expressive manner.

Toto ran to get the gingerbread; and for some time sounds of crunching and nibbling were the only ones that were heard, except the constant "click, click," of the grandmother's needles. Bruin sat for some time watching in silence the endless crossing and re-crossing of the shining bits of steel. Presently he said in a timid growl,—

"Excuse me, ma'am; do you make the gingerbread with those things?"

"With what things, Mr. Bruin?" asked the grandmother.

"Those bright things that go clickety-clack," said the bear. "I see some soft brown stuff on them, just about the color of the gingerbread, and I thought possibly—"

"Oh," said the grandmother, smiling, "you mean my knitting. No, Mr. Bruin, gingerbread is made in a very different way. I mix it in a bowl, with a spoon, and then I put it in a pan, and bake it in the oven. Do you understand?"

Poor Bruin rubbed his nose, and looked helplessly at Coon. The latter, however, merely grinned diabolically at him, and said nothing; so he was obliged to answer the grandmother himself.

"Oh, of course," he said. "If you mix it with a *spoon*, I should say certainly. As far as a spoon goes, you know, I—ah—quite correct, I'm sure." Here the poor fellow subsided into a vague murmur, and glared savagely at the raccoon.

But now the gentle wood-pigeon interposed, with her soft, cooing voice. "Toto," she said, "were we not promised two stories to-day? Tell us the other one now, dear boy, for the shadows are beginning to lengthen."

"I made this story myself, too," said Toto, "and it is called

THE AMBITIOUS ROCKING-HORSE.

There was once a rocking-horse, but he did not want to be a rocking-horse. He wanted to be a trotter. So he went to a jockey—

"What's a jockey?" inquired the bear.

A man who drives fast and tells lies.

He went to a jockey and asked him if he would like to buy a trotter.

"Where is your trotter?" asked the jockey.

"Me's him," said the rocking-horse. That was all the grammar he knew.

"Oh!" said the jockey. "You are the trotter, eh?"

"Yes," said the rocking-horse. "What will you give me for myself?"

"A bushel of shavings," said the jockey.

The rocking-horse thought that was better than nothing, so he sold himself. Then the jockey took him to another jockey who was blind, and told him (the blind jockey) that this was the Sky-born Snorter of the Sarsaparillas, and that he could trot two miles in a minute. So the blind jockey bought him, and paid ten thousand dollars for him.

"'Me's him,' said the rocking-horse."

There was a race the next day, and the blind jockey took the Sky-born Snorter to the race-course, and started him with the other horses. The other horses trotted away round the course, but the Sky-born Snorter stayed just where he was, and rocked; and when the other horses came round the turn, there he was waiting for them at the judge's stand. So he won the race; and the judge gave the prize, which was a white buffalo, to the blind jockey.

The jockey put the Sky-born Snorter in the stable, and then went to get his white buffalo; and while he was gone, the other jockeys came into the stable to see the new horse.

"Why, he's a rocking-horse!" said one of them.

"Hush!" said the Sky-born Snorter. "Yes, I am a rocking-horse, but don't tell my master. He doesn't know it, and he paid ten thousand dollars for me."

"Whom did he pay it to?" asked the jockeys.

"To the other jockey, who bought me from myself," replied the Snorter.

"Oh! and what did *he* give for you?"

"A bushel of shavings," said the Snorter.

"Ah!" said one of the jockeys. "A bushel of shavings, eh? Now, how would you like to have those shavings turned into gold?"

"Very much indeed!" cried the Sky-born.

"Well," said the jockey, "bring them here, and we will change them for you."

So the rocking-horse went and fetched the shavings, and the jockeys set fire to them. The flames shot up, bright and yellow.

"See!" cried the jockeys. "The shavings are all turned into gold. Now we will see what we can do for you." And they took the Sky-born Snorter and put him in the fire, and he turned into gold too, and was all burned up. And the blind jockey drove the white buffalo all the rest of his life, and never knew the difference.

Moral: don't be ambitious.

They all laughed heartily at the fate of the Sky-born Snorter; and the wood-pigeon said, "Both your stories have a most melancholy ending, Toto. One hero boiled and eaten up, and the other burned! It is quite dreadful. I think I must tell the next story myself, and I shall be sure to tell one that ends cheerfully."

"Yes, yes!" cried all the others. "Pigeon Pretty shall be the next story-teller!"

"And now," continued the pigeon, "my Chucky must go home to his supper, for he is not well yet, by any means, and must be very careful of himself. Climb up on Bruin's back, Chucky dear! so, that is right. Good-night, Toto. Good-night, dear madam. Now home again, all!" and flying round and round the bear's head, Pigeon Pretty led the way towards the forest.

CHAPTER VIII.

"IS this one of your own stories that you are going to tell us, Pigeon Pretty?" inquired the squirrel, when they were next assembled around the cottage door.

"No," replied the wood-pigeon. "This is a story I heard a short time ago. I was flying home, after paying a visit to some cousins of mine who live in a village some miles away. As I passed by a pretty white cottage, something like this, I noticed that there were crumbs scattered on one of the window-sills. 'Here lives somebody who is fond of birds!' said I to myself, and as I was rather hungry, I stopped to pick up some of the crumbs. The window was open, and looking in, I saw a pretty and neatly furnished room. Near the window was a bed, in which lay a boy of about Toto's age. He was evidently ill, for he had a bandage tied round his head, and he looked pale and thin. Beside the bed sat a little girl, apparently a year or two older; a sweet, pretty girl, as one would wish to see. She was reading aloud to her brother (I suppose he was her brother) from a large red book. Neither of the children noticed me, so I sat on the window-sill for some time, and heard the whole of this story, which you shall now hear in your turn. It is called

THE STORY OF THE TAIL OF THE BARON'S WAR-HORSE.

Many years ago there lived a Baron, famous in peace and war, but chiefly in the latter. War was his great delight, fighting his natural occupation; and he was never so much in his element as when leading his valiant troops to battle, mounted on his noble iron-gray charger. Ah! what a charger that was!—stately and strong, swift and sure, fiery and bold, yet ready to obey his master's lightest touch or softest word; briefly, a horse in ten thousand. Right proud the Baron was of his gallant steed; and right well did they love each other, horse and master.

The vassals of the Baron knew no greater pleasure than to see their lord ride by mounted on Gray Berold; it filled their souls with joy, and caused them to throw up their caps and shout "Hi!" in a hilarious manner. As for the lovely Ermengarde, the Baron's young and beautiful wife, she would far rather have gone without her dinner than have missed the sight. Whenever Gray Berold was brought to the door, she hastened out, and overwhelmed him with caresses and words of endearment, proffering meanwhile the toothsome sugar and the crisp and sprightly apple, neither of which the engaging animal disdained to accept. In truth, it was a goodly sight to see the golden locks of the lady (for was she not known in all the country as Ermengarde of the Fair

Tresses?) mingling with the wavy silver of the charger's mane as he bent his head lovingly over his fair young mistress,—a goodly sight, and one which often sent the bold Baron rejoicing on his way, with a tender smile on his otherwise slightly ferocious countenance.

It chanced one day that a great tournament was about to take place in the neighborhood. All the knights in the country round, and many bold champions from a greater distance, were to show their prowess in riding at the ring, and in friendly combat with each other. Among the gallant knights, who so ready for the tournament as our bold Baron? He fairly pranced for the fray; for there had been no war for two months, and he was very weary of the long peaceful days. He had been practising for a week past, riding at any number of rings of different sizes, and tilting with his squire, whom he had run through the body several times, thereby seriously impairing that worthy's digestive powers.

And now the eventful morning was come. The vassals were assembled in the courtyard of the castle, a goodly array, to see their master depart in pomp and pride.

Gray Berold was brought round to the door, magnificently caparisoned, his bridle and housings glittering with precious stones. The gallant steed pawed the ground, and tossed his head proudly, as impatient of delay as his master. From a balcony above leaned the lovely Ermengarde, her golden tresses crowned with a nightcap of rare and curious design; for the Baron was making an early start, and his fair lady had not yet completed her toilet.

Amid the vociferous cheers of his vassals, the Baron descended the steps, armed *cap-à-pie*, his good sword by his side, and his mace, battle-axe, cutlass, and shillalah displayed about his stately person in a very imposing manner. He could scarcely walk, it is true, so many and so weighty were his accoutrements; but then, as he himself aptly observed, he did not want to walk.

He got into the saddle with some difficulty, owing to the tendency of his battle-axe to get between his legs; but once there, the warrior was at home. An attendant handed him his lance, with its glittering pennon. Gray Berold pranced and curvetted, making nothing of the enormous weight on his back; the Lady Ermengarde waved her broidered kerchief; and, with a parting glance at his lovely bride, the Baron rode slowly out of the courtyard.

But, alas! he was not destined to ride far. Alas for the proud Baron! Alas and alack for the gallant steed!

He had scarcely ridden a hundred paces when he heard a fearful growl behind him, which caused him to turn quickly in his saddle. What was his horror to see a huge bear spring out of the woods and come rushing towards him!

For one moment the Baron was paralyzed; the next, he wheeled his horse round, and couching his lance, prepared to meet his savage assailant.

"The bear caught the charger by the tail."

But Gray Berold had not bargained for this. Many a fair fight had he seen in battle-field and in tourney; many a time he had faced danger as boldly as his rider, and had borne the brunt of many a fierce attack. But those fights were with men and horses. He knew what they were, and how they should be met; but this was something very different. This great creature, that came rushing along with its head down and its mouth open, was something Berold did not know; moreover, it was something he did not like. Stand there and be rushed at by a thing that was neither horse nor man? Not if he knew it! And just when the bear was close upon him, Gray Berold, with a squeal of mingled terror and anger, wheeled short round. The bear made a spring, and caught the charger by the tail. The terrified animal bounded forward; the Baron made a downward stroke with his battle-axe that would have felled an ox, and Master Bruin (no offence to you, my dear fellow! it's the name of all your family, you know) rolled over and over in the dust.

But alas! and alas! *he took the tail with him!* That noble tail, the pride of the stable-yard, the glory of the grooms, lay in the road, a glittering mass of silver; and it was a tailless steed that now galloped frantically back into the castle-court, from which only a few short minutes ago he had so proudly emerged.

The Baron was mad with fury. Pity for his gallant horse, rage and mortification at the ridiculous plight he was in, anxiety lest he should be late for the tournament, all combined to make him for a time beside himself; he rushed up and down the courtyard, whirling his battle-axe round his head, and uttering the most fearful imprecations. Finally, however, yielding to the tears and entreaties of his retainers, he calmed his noble frenzy, and set himself to think what was best to be done. "Give up the tournament? Perish the thought! Ride another horse than Berold? Never while he lives! Ride him tailless and unadorned? Shades of my ancestors forbid!" thus cried the Baron at every new suggestion of his sympathizing retainers.

At last the head groom had an idea. "Let us fasten on another tail," he said, "an't please your worship!"

"Ha!" cried the Baron, starting at the notion. "'Tis well! Ho! there, Hodge, Barnaby, Perkin! Cut me the tails from the three cart-horses, and tie them together. And be quick about it, ye knaves!"

The three grooms flew to execute their master's mandate, and returned in a few minutes, bearing a magnificent tail, whose varied hues of black, sorrel, and white, showed it to be the spoil of Dobbin, Smiler, and Bumps, the three stout Flemish cart-horses.

"By my halidome, a motley tail!" exclaimed the Baron. "But it boots not, so it be a tail! Fasten it on with all speed, for time presses!—ha! what is this!"

Well might the Baron start, and exclaim.

The moment the three grooms touched the flanks of Gray Berold, before they had time to lay hands on the stump of his tail, they found themselves flying through the air, and tumbling in a very uncomfortable sort of way against the wall of the courtyard. Marry, that was a brave kick! and when he had given it, the charger looked round after the unhappy grooms, and tossed his stately head, and snorted, evidently meaning to say, "*Don't* you want to try it again?"

But the grooms did not want to try it again. They picked themselves up, and rubbed their poor shins and their poor heads, and proceeded to hobble off on their poor feet as fast as they could. But they did not hobble far, for the voice of the Baron was heard in angry expostulation.

"They found themselves flying through the air."

"How now, varlets!" cried that nobleman. "Do you slink away like beaten hounds because, forsooth, the good beast shakes off a fly, or lashes out his heels in playful sport? Shame on ye, coward hinds! Back, I command ye, and tie me on that tail. Obey, sirrahs, or else—hum—ha—hrrrrugh!!!" and the Baron waved his battle-axe, and looked as if he had swallowed the meat-chopper and the gridiron and the blunderbuss, all at one mouthful.

Hodge, Barnaby, and Perkin were in a bad way, assuredly. On the one hand was the charger, snorting defiance, and with his heels all ready for the next kick, should they presume to touch him; on the other was the furious Baron, also snorting, and with his battle-axe all ready for the next whack, should they presume *not* to touch him. Here were two sharp horns to a dilemma!

Cautiously the poor knaves crept up once more behind Gray Berold. "Vault thou upon his back, Perkin!" whispered Barnaby. "Perchance from there—" Whizz! whack! thud!—This time Berold did not wait for them to touch him: the sound of their voices was enough; there they all lay again in a heap against the wall, moaning sore and cursing the day they were born.

But now the Baron's humor changed. "Beshrew me!" he cried. "'Tis a gallant steed. He will not brook, at such a moment, the touch of hireling hands. 'Tis well! give *me* the tail, my masters! and ye shall see."

Alas! they did see; they saw their Baron rolling over and over on the ground. They saw their Baron roll; they heard their Baron rave; they turned and fled for their lives.

At this moment the portal swung open, and the Lady Ermengarde appeared. She had seen all from an upper window, and she now hastened to raise her fallen lord, who sat spluttering and cursing on the ground, unable to rise, owing to the weight of his armor. "Oh! blame not the steed!" cried the lovely lady. "Chide not the gallant beast, good my lord! 'twas not the touch, 'twas the *tail*, he could not brook. Tie the rustic tail of a plebeian cart-horse on Gray Berold? Oh! fie, my lord! it may not be. *I* will provide a tail for your charger!"

"You!" exclaimed the Baron. "What mean you, lady?"

The Lady Ermengarde replied by drawing from the embroidered pouch which hung from her jewelled girdle a pair of shears. Snip! snap! snip! snap! and before her astonished lord could interfere, the golden tresses, the pride of the whole country-side, were severed from her head. Deftly she tied the shining curls together; lightly she stepped to where Gray Berold stood. She stroked his noble head; she spoke to him; she showed him the tresses, and told him what she had done. Then with her own hands she tied them on to the stump of his tail with her embroidered girdle; and Gray Berold moved not fore-leg nor hind, but stood like a steed of granite till it was done.

The retainers were dissolved in tears; the Baron sobbed aloud as he climbed, with the assistance of seven hostlers, into the saddle; but the heroic lady smiled, and bade them be of good cheer. She could get a black wig, she said; and she had always thought she should look better as a brunette.

And to make a long story short, said the wood-pigeon, she *did* get a black wig, and looked like a beauty in it. And the Baron went to the tournament, and won all the prizes. And Gray Berold lived to be sixty years old, and wore the golden tail to the end of his days. And that's all.

CHAPTER IX

"OH! what a delightful story, Pigeon Pretty!" cried Toto. "Did you hear any more like it? I wish I had that red book! Did the boy look as nice as his sister? What was his name?"

"His name," said the pigeon, "was Jim, I think. And he did not—no, Toto, he certainly did *not* look as nice as his sister. In fact, although I pitied him because he was ill, I thought he looked like a disagreeable sort of boy."

"Red hair?" interposed the squirrel, looking at the raccoon.

"Freckled face?" asked the raccoon, looking at the squirrel.

"Why, yes!" said the pigeon, in surprise. "He *had* red hair and a freckled face; but how should you two know anything about him?"

The squirrel and the raccoon nodded at each other.

"Same boy, I should say!" said Cracker.

"Same boy, *I* should say!" answered Coon.

"What is it?" asked Toto, curious as usual. "Tell us about it, one of you! It is early yet, and we have plenty of time."

"Well, I will tell you," said the squirrel. "I meant to keep it and tell it next time, for I cannot make up stories as easily as some of you, and this is something that really happened; but I might just as well tell it now, especially as Pigeon Pretty has told you about the boy.

"You need not be at all sorry for that boy," he continued. "He is a bad boy, and he deserves all he got, and more too."

"Dear, dear!" said the grandmother. "I am sorry to hear that. What did he do, Mr. Cracker?"

"He tried to rob my Uncle Munkle of his winter store!" replied the squirrel. "And he got the worst of it, that's all."

"Who is your Uncle Munkle?" asked Toto. "I don't know him, do I?"

"No," said Cracker. "He lives quite at the other end of the wood, where people sometimes go for fagots and nuts and such things. Nobody ever comes near our end of the wood, because they are afraid of Bruin.

"My uncle is a Munk," he continued, "and a most excellent person."

"A monk?" interrupted the grandmother in amazement.

"Yes, a Chipmunk!" said the squirrel. "It's the same thing, I believe, only we spell it with a *u*. Third cousin to a monkey, you know."

Toto and his grandmother both looked quite bewildered at this; but the raccoon smiled sweetly, and said,—

"Go on, Cracker, my boy! never try to explain things *too* fully; it's apt to be a little tedious, and it is always better to leave something to the imagination."

"I am going on," said Cracker. "As I said before, people sometimes go into that part of the wood; there are one or two hives not far from it."

"One or two hives?" interrupted Toto. "What *do* you mean, Cracker?"

"Why, a lot of houses together," said the squirrel. "Don't you call them hives? The only other creatures I know that live in that kind of way (and a very poor way it is, to my thinking) are the bees, and their places are called hives."

"A collection of houses, Mr. Cracker," said the grandmother gently, "is called a village or a town, according to its size; a village being a small collection."

"Oh!" said the squirrel. "Thank you, ma'am! I will try to remember that. Well, this boy Jim lives in the nearest village, and sometimes goes into the forest. Now, the autumn is slipping away fast, as we all know; and last week my Uncle Munkle, who is always fore-handed and thrifty, thought it was high time to be getting in his winter store of nuts and acorns. So he sent for his nephews to come and help him (he has no children of his own). We all went, of course, and Coon went with us, for my uncle always gives us a feast after the nuts are in, and Coon always goes wherever there is anything to—"

"What?" said the raccoon, looking up sharply.

"Wherever there is anything to be *done!*" said the squirrel hastily.

"The second day, as we were all hard at work shelling the beechnuts, I heard a noise among the bushes,—a crackling noise that did not sound like any animal I knew. I looked, and saw two eyes peering out from the leaves of a young beech-tree. 'That is a boy,' said I to myself, 'and he means mischief!' So I skipped off without saying anything to the others, and crept softly round behind the bushes, making no more noise than an eel in the mud. There I found, not one boy, but two, crouching among the bushes, and watching the nut-shelling. They were whispering to each other; and I crept nearer and nearer till I could hear all they said.

"'When shall we come?' said one.

"'To-night,' said the other, who had red hair and a freckled face, 'when the moon is up, and the little beggars are all asleep. Then we can easily knock them on the head, and get the nuts without being bitten. They bite like wild-cats when they are roused, these little fellows.'

"'All right!' said the other, whose face I could not see. 'I'll bring a bag and be here at eight o'clock.'

"'*Will* you?' thought I, and I crept away again, having heard all I wanted to know. I went back to the others, and presently a snapping and crackling told me that the boys were gone. Then I went to Uncle Munkle and told him what I had heard. He was very angry, and whisked his tail about till he nearly whisked it off. 'Call your large friend,' he said, 'and we will hold a council.' So I waked Coon—"

"Waked Coon?" exclaimed the woodchuck slyly. "What! do you mean to say he was not working twice as hard as any of the others?"

"I had been, my good fellow!" said the raccoon loftily. "I had been; and exhausted with my labors. I was snatching a moment's hard-earned repose. Go on, Cracker."

"Well," continued the squirrel, "we held a council, and settled everything beautifully. Uncle Munkle, who has very particularly sharp teeth, was to get into the nut-closet and wait there. The rest of us were to be ready together on the nearest branch, and Coon was to hide himself somewhere close by. No one was to move until Uncle Munkle gave the signal, and then—well, you shall hear how it happened. We all went on with our work until sunset. Then we had supper, and a game of scamper, and then we began to prepare for business. We sharpened our claws on the bark of the trees till they were as sharp as—as—"

"Razors," suggested Toto.

"Don't know what that means," said the squirrel.

"As sharp as Coon's nose, then; that will do."

"We filled our cheek-pouches with three-cornered pebbles and nut-shells. Then, when the moon rose, and all the forest was quiet, we retired to our posts. We had waited some time, and were becoming rather impatient, when suddenly a distant sound was heard; the sound of snapping and cracking twigs. It grew louder and louder, louder and louder; and presently we saw a freckled face looking out from among the leaves.

"Cautiously the boy advanced, and soon another boy appeared, not so ill-looking as the first. He carried a bag in his hand. The two came softly to the foot of our tree, and looked up. The leaves twinkled in the moonlight; but all was still, not a sound to be heard. The two whispered together a moment; then the freckled boy began slowly and carefully to climb the tree. We saw his red head coming nearer and nearer, nearer and nearer. We knew he must be near Uncle Munkle's hole. We all held our breath and listened for the signal.

"Presently the boy stopped climbing, and we saw him stretch out his hand. Then—oh! such a screech! You *never* heard such a screech, not even from a wild-cat. Another yell, and another. That was the signal. Now we knew what Uncle Munkle meant by saying, 'I may not give the signal *myself*, but you will hear it all the same.'

"Instantly we sprang at the boy, ten strong, healthy squirrels, teeth and claws and all. I don't think he enjoyed himself very much for the next few minutes. He yelled all the time, and at last he lost his hold on the tree, and fell heavily to the ground. Also, Coon had been biting his legs a little. But when he fell, Coon started after the other boy, who was dancing about the foot of the tree in a frenzy of terror and amazement. When he saw Coon coming, he started on a run; but Coon jumped on his back and got him by the ear, and then rode him round and round the forest till he howled as loud as the other one had."

"A very pleasant ride I had, too," said the raccoon placidly. "My young friend was excitable, very excitable, but that only made it the more lively. Yes. I don't know when I have enjoyed anything more."

"But what became of the first boy after he fell?" asked Toto eagerly.

65

"His father took him away in a wheelbarrow."

"Well, my dear, he lay still," said the squirrel. "He lay still. He had broken his leg, so it was really the only thing for him to do. And when Coon came back from riding the other boy he jumped backwards and forwards over him till his father came and took him away in a wheelbarrow. Every time Coon jumped, he grinned at the boy; and every time he grinned, the boy screamed; so one inferred that he did not like it, you know.

"Altogether," said the little squirrel, in conclusion, "it was a great success; a great success; really, worthy of our end of the wood. And *such* a feast as Uncle Munkle gave us the day after!"

65

CHAPTER X.

IT was agreed by all hands at the next meeting, that Bruin must tell the story.

"You have not told a story for a long, long time, Bruin," said Toto,—"not since we began to meet here; and Granny wants to hear one of your stories; don't you, Granny?"

"Indeed," said the grandmother, "I should like very much to hear one of Mr. Bruin's stories. I am told they are very delightful."

Mr. Bruin bowed in his peculiar fashion, and murmured something which sounded like "How-wow-mumberygrubble."

The old lady knew, however, that it was meant for "Thank you, ma'am," and took the will for the deed.

Bruin sucked his paw thoughtfully for a few minutes; then, raising his head with an air of inspiration,—"Pigeon Pretty," he asked, "what kind of a bear was that in your story?"

"Really, Bruin, I do not know," replied the wood-pigeon. "It said 'a bear,' that was all."

"You see," continued Bruin, "there are so many kinds of bears,—black, brown, cinnamon, grizzly, polar,—really, there is no end to them. I thought, however, that this might possibly have been the Lost Prince of the Poles."

Here Bruin paused a moment and looked about.

"The Lost Prince of the Poles!" exclaimed Toto. "What a fine name for a story! Tell us now, Bruin; tell us all about him."

"Listen, then," said the bear, "and you shall hear about

THE LOST PRINCE OF THE POLES.

The polar bears, as you probably know, are a large and powerful nation. They are governed by a king, who is called the Solar-Polarity of the Hypopeppercorns.

"Oh!" cried Toto. "What *does* that mean?"

66

Nobody knows what it means. That is the great charm of the title. Gives it majesty, you understand. The present Solar-Polarity is, I am told, quite worthy of his title, for he is very majestic, and knows absolutely nothing. He sits on the top of the North Pole, and directs the movement of the icebergs.

At the time of which I am going to tell you, which was so long ago as to be no particular time at all, the Solar-Polarity had an only son,—a most promising young bear,—the heir to the kingdom. He was brought up with the greatest care possible, and when he had arrived at a suitable age, his father begged him to choose a mate among the youngest and fairest of the she-bears, or, as they are more elegantly termed, bearesses. To the amazement of the Solar-Polarity, the Prince flatly refused.

"I will not marry one of these cold, white creatures!" he said; "I am tired of white. I want to marry one of those things;" and he pointed to the north, where the Northern Lights were shooting up in long streamers of crimson and green and purple.

"One of those things!" cried his father. "My dear son, are you mad? Those are Rory-Bories; they are not the sort of thing one can marry. It's—it's ridiculous to think of such a thing."

"Well," said the Prince, "then I will marry the creature that is most like them. There must be some creature that has those pretty colors. I will go and ask the Principal Whale."

So he went and asked the Principal Whale if he knew any creature that was colored like the Rory-Bories.

"Frankly," said the whale, "I do not. Doubtless there are such, but I have never happened to meet any of them. I will tell you what I will do, however," he said, seeing the Prince's look of disappointment. "I am just starting on a voyage to the Southern seas; and if you like I will take you with me, and you can look about you and decide for yourself."

The young bear was delighted with this proposition, and proceeded at once to assume the full-dress costume of the polar bears, which consists in tying three knots in the tail.

"A—*excuse* me!" interrupted the raccoon, "I thought no bears had any tails to speak of;" and he glanced complacently at his own magnificent tail, which was curled round his feet.

"He sailed away for the Southern seas."

They have none to speak of; which makes it all the more remarkable for them to be able to tie three knots in them. As soon as this was accomplished, the Prince declared that he was ready to start.

"So am I," said the Principal Whale. And taking the Prince of the Poles on his back, he sailed away for the Southern seas.

They went on and on for several days without any adventures; till one day the young bear saw a huge jelly-fish floating towards them. "See!" he cried, "there is a lovely creature, as bright and beautiful as the Rory-Bories. Surely this is the creature for me to marry!"

"I don't think you would like to marry that," said the whale. "That is a jelly-fish. But we will go and speak to it, and you can judge for yourself." So the whale swam up to the jelly-fish, who looked at them, but said nothing.

"My dear," said the Prince, "you are very beautiful."

"Yah!" said the jelly-fish (who was in reality extremely ignorant, and had never gone to dancing-school), "that's more than I can say for you!"

"I am sorry to hear you say that," said the Prince, mildly.

"Will you marry me, and be Princess of the Poles?"

"Marry your grandmother!" replied the jelly-fish in a very rude manner; and off it flounced under the water.

The young bear looked sadly after it. "It was very pretty," he said; "why did it want me to marry my grandmother?"

"It didn't," replied the whale. "That was only its way of speaking. An unmannerly minx! Don't think any more about it," and they continued their voyage.

A couple of days after this they met the swordfish and his daughter.

"These are some friends of mine," said the Principal Whale. "We will see if they can aid us in our search."

The swordfish greeted them kindly, and invited them to come down and make him a visit.

"Thank you," said the whale. "We have not time to stop now. We are in search of a creature as bright in color as the Rory-Bories. My young friend here, the Prince of the Poles, is anxious to marry such a creature, if he can only find her."

But the swordfish shook his head, and said he could not think of any one who would answer the description.

"*I* will marry you if you wish," said the swordfish's daughter, who was much struck by the appearance of the young bear. "I am considered very agreeable, and I think I could make you happy."

"But you are not bright," cried the poor Prince in distress. "You are even black, saving your presence. I don't wish to hurt your feelings, but really you are not at all the sort of creature I was looking for; though I have no doubt," he added, "that you are extremely agreeable."

"You might play I was a Rory-Bory behind a cloud on a dark night," suggested the swordfish's daughter.

But the Prince did not think that would do, and the whale agreed with him. "One cannot play," he said, "when one is married." Accordingly they bade a friendly farewell to the swordfish and his daughter, and continued their voyage.

After several days they saw in the distance the coast of Africa. As they approached it, the Prince saw something bright on the land, near the edge of the water. "See!" he cried, "there is something very bright and beautiful. Let us go nearer, and see what it is." So they went nearer, and saw a long line of scarlet flamingoes, drawn up on the beach like a company of soldiers.

"Prince," said the Principal Whale, "your journey has not been in vain. I really think these are the creatures you have been looking for."

As he spoke, the flamingoes, who had caught sight of the strange creatures approaching the shore, rose into the air, with a great flapping of wings, and flew slowly away.

The Prince was in ecstasies. "Oh, Whale!" he cried, "these *are* Rory-Bories, real live Rory-Bories! See how they shoot up, like long streamers! See how they glow and shine! One still remains on the shore, the loveliest of all. She is my bride! She is the Princess of the Poles! Swim close to the shore, good Whale!"

The whale swam up to the shore, the water being fortunately deep enough to allow him to do so, and the bear addressed the solitary flamingo, which still stood upon the beach, watching them with great curiosity. This was, in fact, the Princess of the Flamingoes; and besides being rather curious by nature, she thought it would be beneath her dignity to fly away just because some strange creatures were approaching. So she stood still, in an attitude of royal ease.

"Lovely creature!" said the Prince, "tell me, oh, tell me, are you really and truly a Rory-Bory? I am sure you must be, from your brilliant and exquisite beauty."

"Not quite," answered the flamingo. "Not *quite* the same thing, though very nearly. I am a flamingo, and the Rory-Bory is a flaming go; pronounced differently, you perceive. That is the principal difference between the two families, though there are some other minor variations, which may be caused by the climate. What is your pleasure with me, and what might you happen to be?"

"My pleasure is to marry you!" exclaimed the young bear rapturously. "I am a white bear, and am called the Prince of the Poles. After my father's death I shall become Solar-Polarity of the Hypopeppercorns. Will you be my bride, and reign with me as queen? You shall sit upon the North Pole, and direct the movements of the icebergs."

The flamingo closed one eye, and drew up one leg in an attitude of graceful and maidenly coyness. "Your manners and bearing interest me much," she said after a pause; "and I should be glad to do as you suggest, but I fear it is impossible. We are not allowed to marry any one with more than two legs; and you, I perceive, have four."

The poor Prince was quite staggered by this remark, for he was proud of his legs, which, though short, were finely formed. He was silent in dismay. But now the Principal Whale interposed. "Would it not be possible to make an exception in this case?" he asked. "My young friend has come a very long way in search of you, and has quite set his heart on this marriage."

"Alas!" said the flamingo, "I fear not. It is the first law in the kingdom, and I dare not break it."

"What shall I do, then?" cried the Prince in despair. "If I cannot have you, I will go back and marry the swordfish's daughter, and you would be sorry to have me do that if you knew how ugly she was."

"In difficult cases," said the flamingo, "we always consult the hippopotamouse. I should advise you to do the same."

"The hippopotamouse?" exclaimed the Prince. "Where is he to be found? Tell me, that I may fly to him at once."

"He lives in the middle of the central plain of Pongolia," replied the flamingo.

"In that case," said the Principal Whale, "I must leave you, my Prince, as travelling on land is one of the pleasures I must deny myself, being constitutionally unfitted for it."

The Prince thanked the whale warmly for his kindness, and after taking a most affecting leave of the Flamingo Princess, he set off for the central plain of Pongolia.

He travelled night and day, and after many days he arrived at the very middle of the plain. There he found the hippopotamouse, sitting in the middle of a river, nibbling a huge cheese.

This singular animal combined all the chief qualities of a hippopotamus and a mouse. His appearance was truly astonishing, and filled the mind of the Prince with mingled feelings. He stood for some time gazing at him in silent amazement.

Presently the hippopotamouse looked up sharply. "Well," he said, "what do you want? Do you think I am pretty?"

"N-no!" replied the young bear. "You may be good; but I don't think you are pretty. I want," he continued, "to marry the Flamingo Princess. I am the Prince of the Poles, son of the Solar-Polarity of the Hypopeppercorns. You may have heard of my father."

"Oh! ah! yes!" said the hippopotamouse. "I've heard of *him*. Well, why *don't* you marry her?"

"Because I have four legs," answered the Prince sadly; "and it is against the law for a flamingo to marry any one with more than two."

"True. I had forgotten that," said the hippopotamouse.

"Can you suggest any way out of the difficulty?" inquired the Prince.

Without making any reply, the hippopotamouse plunged into meditation and the cheese at the same moment, and nibbled and meditated in silence for several hours; while the unhappy Prince stood first on one leg, and then on the other, endeavoring in vain to conceal his impatience. Finally, when he was quite exhausted with waiting, the hippopotamouse took his head out of the cheese.

"My young friend," he said, "I see but one way."

"My young friend," he said, "I see but one way out of the difficulty, and that is for you to walk about on two of your legs until they are worn out. Then, you perceive, you will have, unless my calculations have misled me, exactly two left,—the proper number to enable you legally to marry the Flamingo Princess. You may find this fatiguing," he continued, seeing the Prince's look of dismay; "but really I can see nothing else for you to do; and when you reflect that everything is more or less fatiguing, and that I have worn out five complete sets of teeth on this very cheese, you may become reconciled to your lot. Good-by. I wish you well." And without more ado, he plunged into the cheese once more.

The unhappy Prince uttered one wild howl, and turning away, fled into the savage wilds of the Pongolian forest.

Here Bruin paused, shook his head, and sighed deeply.

"Oh! go on, Bruin," cried Toto eagerly. "How *can* you stop there? Go on immediately, and tell us the rest!"

Alas! there is little more to tell; for from that moment the Prince of the Poles has never been seen or heard of.

The Flamingo Princess waited long and anxiously for his return; but he never came. I believe she finally married an ostrich, who led her a terrible life.

The Principal Whale called at the coast of Africa on his way back from the Southern seas, and hearing the sad intelligence of the Prince's disappearance, departed in great sadness for his Northern home, to break the news to the

Solar-Polarity of the Hypopeppercorns. When that potentate heard of the disappearance of his son, he fell off the North Pole, and broke his neck; and the whole nation assumed the mourning costume of the polar bears, which consists in tying a sailor's knot in the left ear, and a granny's knot in the right.

And thus ends, in sadness and despair, the story of "The Lost Prince of the Poles."

CHAPTER XI

ONE afternoon (it was not a "story" afternoon, for the grandmother was very busy, dyeing some of her homespun yarn) Toto went off to the forest early, intending to have a game of scamper with Coon and Cracker. As he sauntered along with his hands in his pockets, he met the woodchuck. Master Chucky looked very spruce and neat, and was trotting along with an air of great self-satisfaction.

"Hallo! you Chucky," exclaimed Toto, "where are you going?"

The woodchuck stopped, and glanced around with his sharp little eyes. "Is any one with you, Toto?" he asked,—"Coon, or Cracker, or any of those fellows?"

"No," answered Toto in some surprise. "I was just going to find them. Do you want them?"

"No, indeed!" exclaimed the woodchuck. "You see," and he lowered his voice confidentially, "I am going to a rinktum, and I don't want those fellows to know about it."

"What is a rinktum?" asked Toto. "And why don't you want them to know about it?"

"Why, a rinktum is a rabbit's ball, of course. What else should it be?" answered Chucky. "The rabbits have invited me; but at the last one Coon ate up all the supper, and bit the rabbits if they tried to get any; so they determined not to invite him again, and asked me not to say anything about it."

"Oh, Chucky," exclaimed Toto, "I wish you would take me! I have never been to a rabbit's ball, and I should like to go *so* much! and I wouldn't eat anything at all!" he added, seeing that the woodchuck looked doubtful.

Chucky brightened up at the last remark, and said, "Well, after all, I don't see why I shouldn't take you. They are always glad to see people, if they will only behave themselves. So come along, Toto;" and the fat little creature hurried along, with Toto following him.

"You may have some difficulty," he said as they went along, "in getting into the ball-room, but I think you will be able to squeeze through. It is in the Big Burrow, which is certainly large enough for any reasonable creature. Here we are now at the mouth of the burrow."

They were crossing a rough, uneven meadow, with trees and shrubs thickly scattered over it; and the woodchuck stopped at a large juniper-bush, in front of which sat a black rabbit.

"How do you do, Woodchuck?" inquired the rabbit. "And who is this with you?"

"This is a—a—a boy, in fact," said the woodchuck in some embarrassment. "He is a great friend of mine, and has never seen a rinktum in his life, so I ventured to bring him. He—he won't eat anything!" he added in a whisper.

The rabbit bowed to Toto by way of reply, and pulling aside the branches of the juniper-bush, disclosed a large hole in the ground.

"Follow me," said the woodchuck; "I will lead the way." And he disappeared through the mouth of the hole.

Toto dropped on his hands and knees, and followed as best he could. The path was *very* narrow, and wound about and about in a very inconvenient manner. Several times the boy was stuck so fast that it seemed as if he *could not* get any farther; but he always managed, by much wriggling, to squeeze through the tight places. It was perfectly dark, but there was no possibility of his losing his way, for obvious reasons. At last he saw a glimmer of light ahead. It grew brighter and brighter; and at last Toto emerged from the passage, and found himself in a large cave, which in one part was high enough to allow him to stand upright. He immediately crawled over to this part, and getting on his feet, looked about at the strange scene before him.

The Big Burrow was lighted by the United Company of Glow-worms. These little creatures had arranged themselves in patterns all over the walls and roof of the cave, and were shining with all their might. The effect was truly lovely, and Toto could not help wishing that his grandmother's cottage were lighted in the same way. The floor was crowded with rabbits of every size and color, and they were all dancing. Black rabbits, brown rabbits, white rabbits, big and little rabbits, racing round and round, jumping up and down, shaking their ears, and wiggling their noses. Oh, what a good time they were having!

"Would you like to dance?" asked a very large white rabbit, who seemed to be the master of ceremonies, looking up at Toto.

"Thank you," said Toto. "I do not know the step, and I should only make confusion among the dancers, I fear."

"Oh, you will have no difficulty in learning the step," said the white rabbit. "Nothing could be easier: first you jump up, then wriggle your hind-legs in the air, then turn round three times, rub your nose with your right fore-paw, jump again, rub your nose with your left hind-paw, turn round—"

"But I have only two legs," objected Toto meekly.

"Would you like to dance?"

"Dear, dear!" said the master of ceremonies. "That does seem to be a difficulty, doesn't it? What a pity! Haven't you ever had any more?"

"No," said Toto. "We are not made that way, you see. But don't mind me," he added, seeing that the hospitable rabbit seemed really distressed. "I only came to look on, and I am enjoying myself very much indeed, I assure you."

"Pretty sight, isn't it, Toto?" said the woodchuck, bustling up, while the master of ceremonies went off to attend to his duties. "See that young white rabbit with the black nose and tail? She is the belle of the evening, I should say. Lovely creature! I have just danced twice with her."

"What *is* that brown rabbit doing?" exclaimed Toto. "He has been standing on his head before her, and now he is lying on his back and kicking his feet in the air. I think he is in a fit."

"No, no," said the woodchuck. "Oh, no. He is merely expressing his devotion to her, that is all. He has been in love with her for a long time," he added, "but I don't think it will ever come to anything. He has no whiskers to speak of, and he comes from a very inferior sort of burrow. She ought not to dance with him at all, in point of fact, but she is *so* amiable!"

"It is a pity they have no music," said Toto. "I don't see how they manage to dance. Would they like me to whistle for them, do you think, Chucky?"

"Oh, *wouldn't* they!" cried the woodchuck in delight. "What a nice boy you are, Toto! I am *so* glad I brought you!"

So Toto whistled a merry tune, and the rabbits nearly went mad with delight. They capered, and jumped, and wriggled their hind-legs, and rubbed their noses, till Toto really thought they would dance themselves into small pieces; and when he stopped, they all tumbled down on the ground in little black and white and brown heaps, and lay panting and exhausted.

The master of ceremonies came up to Toto, and after making him nine very polite bows, thanked him warmly for the pleasure he had given them. "This is certainly *the* rinktum of the season," he said, "and much of its success is owing to your kindness." He then begged Toto to come into the supper-room, and led the way to an adjoining cave.

Toto followed, with a comical glance at the woodchuck, to remind him that he had not forgotten his promise.

The supper was served in superb style, worthy of "*the* rinktum of the season." There was cabbage-soup and broccoli broth. There were turnips and carrots, celery and beets and onions, in profusion; and in the centre of the room rose a lofty mountain of crisp green lettuce. Ah! that was a supper to do a rabbit's heart good!

Toto, mindful of his promise, showed great self-denial with regard to the raw vegetables, and even remained firm against the attractions of the cabbage-soup.

The white rabbit was quite melancholy over his guest's persistent refusal to eat of his good cheer. "But perhaps," he said, "creatures of your race never eat. I see that your nose does not wiggle when you speak, so perhaps you cannot eat, eh?"

"Oh, yes," said Toto in an off-hand way. "Yes, we *can*; and sometimes we *do*. I have eaten in the course of my life, and I may do it again, but not to-night."

At this moment the guests all came pouring into the supper-room; and Toto began to think that it would be wise for him to slip away quietly, as it must be near his own supper-time, and his grandmother would be wondering where he was. So he took a friendly leave of the master of ceremonies, and nodding to the woodchuck, he left the supper-room, made his way through the ball-room, and dropping once more on his hands and knees, proceeded to wriggle his way as best he might through the underground passage.

A very grimy and dusty boy he was when he came out again from behind the juniper-bush. He shook himself as well as he could, laughed a little over the recollection of the unsuccessful rabbit suitor kicking his heels in the air to express his devotion, and started on his way home.

He had spent a much longer time than he had meant to at the rinktum, and it was growing quite dark. He hurried along, for his way lay through a part of the wood where he did not like to go after dark. The owls lived there, and Toto did not like the owls, because none of his friends liked them. They were surly, growly, ill-tempered birds, and were apt to make themselves very disagreeable if one met them after dark. Indeed, it was said that Mrs. Growler, the old grandmother owl of the family, had once eaten several of Cracker's brothers and sisters. The squirrel did not like to talk about it, but Toto knew that he hated the owls bitterly.

"I hope I shall not meet any of them," said the boy to himself as he entered the wood. "I am not afraid of them, of course,—it would be absurd for a boy to be afraid of an owl,—but I don't like them."

The thought had scarcely crossed his mind, when he heard a sound of flapping wings; and a moment after a huge white owl flew down directly in front of him, and spreading its broad pinions, completely barred his passage.

"Who?" said the owl.

"'Who?' said the owl. 'Toto,' said the boy."

"Toto," said the boy shortly. "Let me pass, please. I'm in a hurry."

"You're late!" said the owl severely.

"I know it," replied Toto. "That's why I asked you to let me pass. I don't want to talk to you, Mrs. Growler, and I don't suppose you want to talk to me."

"Whit!" cried Mrs. Growler (for it was no other than that redoubtable female). "Don't give me any of your impudence, sir! What do you mean by coming into our wood after dark, and then insulting me? Here, Hoots! Flappy! Horner! Come here, all of you! Here's this imp of a boy who's always making mischief here with that thieving raccoon. Let us give him a lesson, and teach him to stay where he belongs, and not come spying and prying into our wood!"

Immediately a rushing sound was heard from all sides, and half-a-dozen owls came hooting and screaming around our hero.

Toto held his ground manfully, though he saw that the odds were greatly against him. One owl was all very well; but seven or eight owls, all armed with powerful beaks and claws, and all angry, were quite another matter, especially as the darkness, which exactly suited them, made it difficult for him to tell in which direction he should beat his retreat, supposing he were able to beat it at all.

He set his back against a tree, and faced the hooting, flapping crowd, whose great round eyes glared fiercely at him.

"I've never done any harm to any of you," he said boldly. "I've never thrown stones at you, and I've never taken more than one egg at a time from your nests. You have always hated me, Mother Growler, because I am a friend of Coon; and you're afraid of Coon, you know you are. Come, let me go home quietly, and I'll promise not to come into your part of the wood again.

"I'm sure, there's no inducement for coming," he added in a lower tone. "It's the scraggiest part of the whole forest,—only fit for owls to live in!"

"Hoo! hoo!" cried Mother Growler in a rage. "I'm afraid of Coon, am I? A nasty, thieving creature, with an amount of tail that is simply disgusting! And our wood is scraggy, is it? Hoo! Give it to him, children!"

"Peck him!" cried all the owls in chorus; "scratch him! tear him! hustle him!" and, with wings and claws spread, they came flying at Toto.

Toto put one arm before his face, and prepared to defend himself as well as he could with the other. His blood was up, and he had no thought of trying to escape. If he could only get Mother Growler by the head now, and wring her neck!

But blows were falling like hail on his own head now,—sharp blows from horny beaks and crooked talons. They were tearing his jacket off. He was dazed, almost stunned, by the beating of the huge wings in his face. Decidedly, our Toto is in a bad way.

Suddenly a loud crackling noise was heard among the bushes. It came nearer; it grew louder. Toto listened, with his heart in his mouth. Surely, but one animal there was big enough to make a noise like that.

"*Bruin!*" he cried, with all the breath he could gather, panting and struggling as he was. "Bruin! help! help!"

A portentous growl answered his cry. The boughs crackled and burst right and left, and the next instant the bear sprang through the bushes.

"What is it?" he cried. "Toto, that was your voice. Where are you, boy? What is the matter?"

"Here!" cried Toto faintly. "Here, Bruin! The owls—" But at that moment the little fellow's voice failed, and he sank bleeding and exhausted on the ground.

"How-grrrrr-wow-*wurra*-WURRA-WURRA-WOW!!!"

In two minutes more there were no owls in that part of the wood. Hoots, Horner, and the rest, when they saw the fiery eyes and glittering teeth of the bear, and heard his terrible roar, as he rushed upon them, loosed their hold of the boy, and flew for their lives. As for Mother Growler—

"I *did* say," remarked Bruin, taking some feathers out of his mouth, "that I never would eat another owl unless it was plucked. Feathers are certainly a most inferior article of food; but in a case of this kind it is really the only thing to do. As Coon says, it settles the matter, and there is no further trouble about it. And now," continued the good bear, "how is my dear boy? Why, Toto! look up, boy. They are all gone, and you are cock of the whole wood. Come, my Toto! I'll eat them all, if they have hurt the boy!" he added in an undertone.

But Toto made no reply. He had, in point of fact, fainted from exhaustion and excitement.

Bruin sniffed at him, and poked him from head to foot; then, finding that no bones were broken, he lifted the boy gently by the waistband of his breeches, and shambled off in the direction of the cottage.

CHAPTER XII

THE grandmother all this time was wondering very much where her Toto was. "What can have become of the boy?" she said to herself for the twentieth time. "He is always punctual at supper-time; and now it is more than an hour past. It must be quite dark, too, in the wood. Where can he be?" And she went to the door and listened, as she had been listening ever since six o'clock. "Toto!" she said aloud. "Toto, do you hear me?" But no sound came in reply, save the distant hoot of an owl; and reluctantly the good woman closed the door again, and went back to her knitting. She felt very anxious, very much troubled; but what could she do? Blind and alone, she was quite helpless. Suppose the boy should have wandered off into some distant part of the forest, and lost his way? Suppose he should have encountered some fierce wild beast, unlike the friendly creatures with whom he played every day? Suppose—But here the current of her anxious thoughts was interrupted by a sound; a curious sound,—a soft *thud* against the door, followed by a scratching noise, and a sound of heavy breathing.

The poor grandmother turned cold with fear; she did not dare to move for some minutes; but the thud was repeated several times, as if somebody were trying to knock. She tottered towards the door, and said in a tremulous voice, "Who is there?"

"Only Bruin, ma'am," was the reply, in a meek growl.

Oh, how relieved the grandmother was! With hands that still trembled she unfastened the door. "Oh, Mr. Bruin!" she cried. "Dear Mr. Bruin, I am so glad you have come! Can you tell me anything about Toto? He has not come home, and I am very anxious indeed. I fear he may have met some wild creature, and—"

"Well, ma'am," said the bear slowly, "as for being wild—well, yes; perhaps you *would* call her wild. And I don't say she was amiable, and she was certainly very free in the matter of claws; very free, indeed, she was!"

"What *do* you mean, Mr. Bruin?" cried the poor old lady. "Claws? Oh! then I know he *has* been attacked, and you know all about it, and have come to break it to me. My boy! my boy! Tell me quickly where he is, and what has happened to him!"

"Don't be alarmed, ma'am," said Bruin. "Pray don't be alarmed! there are no bones broken, I assure you; and as for *her*, you need have no further anxiety. I—I saw to the matter myself, and I have no reason to think—no, I really have *no* reason to think that you will have any further trouble with her."

"*Her!*" said the bewildered old grandmother. "I don't—I *can't* understand you, Mr. Bruin. I want to know what has become of Toto, my boy."

"Certainly, certainly," said the bear hastily. "Very natural, I'm sure; don't mention it, I beg of you. As for a little blood, you know," he added apologetically, "that couldn't be helped, you see. I didn't come up quite soon enough; but we know the blood is *there*, after all; and a little of it outside instead of inside,—why, what difference does it make? He has plenty left, you know."

"Bruin, Bruin!" cried a faint voice, "do stop! You will frighten her to death with your explanations. Here I am, Granny dear, safe and sound, barring a few scratches." And Toto, who had been gradually recovering his senses during the last few minutes, raised himself from the doorstep on which the bear had laid him, and flung his arms round his grandmother's neck.

The poor old woman gave a cry of joy, and then burst into tears, being quite overcome by the sudden change from grief and anxiety to security and delight.

At the sight of her tears, the worthy Bruin uttered a remorseful growl, and boxed his own ears several times very severely, assuring himself that he was quite the most stupid beast that ever lived, and that he was always making a mess of it. "I didn't mean to frighten you, ma'am," he said, "I didn't indeed; but I am such a stupid! And now," he added, "I think I must be going. Good-night, ma'am."

"What!" cried Toto, turning from his grandmother, and throwing his arms in turn round the bear's huge shaggy neck. "Going, before we have thanked you? Going off without a word, after saving my life? Oh, you unnatural old Bruin! you shall not stir! Do you know, Granny, that he has saved my life from the owls, and that if it had not been for him you would have no Toto at all, but only a hundred little bits of him?" And he told the whole story in glowing words, while Bruin hung his head and shuffled from one foot to another, much abashed at hearing his own praises.

And when the grandmother had heard all about it, what did she do? Why, she too put her arms round the huge shaggy neck; and if ever a bear came near being hugged to death, it was that bear.

"And now," said the grandmother, when she had recovered her composure, and had thanked and blessed Bruin till he did not know whether he had one head or seven, "it is very late, and I am sure you must be tired. Why will you not stay and spend the night with us? There is a beautiful fire in the kitchen, and a nice soft rug in front of it, on which you could sleep very comfortably. Do stay!"

The bear rubbed his nose and looked helplessly at Toto. "I don't think—" he began.

"Of course he will stay," said Toto decidedly. "There isn't any 'thinking' about it. He will stay. Walk in, old fellow, and sit down in front of the fire, and Granny will give us both some supper. Oh! my Granny dear, if you *knew* how hungry I am!"

It would have been a pleasant sight, had there been any one there to enjoy it, to see the trio gathered around the bright wood-fire an hour later. The grandmother sat in her high-backed arm-chair, in snowy cap and kerchief, knitting and smiling, smiling and knitting, as happy and contented as a grandmother could possibly be. On the other side of the hearth sat the bear, blinking comfortably at the fire, while Toto leaned against his shaggy side, and chattered like a magpie.

"How jolly this is!" he said. "It reminds me of Snow-White and Rose-Red, when the bear came and slept in front of the fire. By the way, Bruin, you are not an enchanted prince, are you? The bear in that story was an enchanted prince. What fun if you should be!"

"Not to my knowledge," replied the bear, shaking his head. "Not—to—my—knowledge. Never heard of such a thing in our branch of the family. I had a cousin once who travelled with a showman, but that is the only thing of the kind that I know of."

"Tell us about your cousin!" said Toto, eager, as usual, for a story. "How came he to take to the show business?"

"The man taught him to beat the drum."

"It took him," said Bruin. "He was taken when he was a little fellow, only a few months old. The man who caught him made a pet of him at first; taught him to dance, and shake paws, and beat the drum. He was a drummer in the army,— the man, I mean. He was very kind, and my cousin grew extremely fond of him."

"What was your cousin's name?" asked Toto.

"They called him 'Grimshaw;'" said Bruin. "His master's name was Shaw, and he was grim, you know, when he didn't like people, and so they called him 'Grimshaw.' He mostly *didn't* like people," added the bear reflectively. "He certainly didn't like the showman."

"Then Shaw was not the showman?" said Toto.

"Oh, dear, no!" said Bruin. "A war broke out, and Shaw's regiment was ordered off, and he couldn't take Grimshaw with him. He was very big then, and the other soldiers didn't like him. He had a way of going into the different tents and taking anything he happened to fancy for supper; and if any one said anything to him, he boxed that one's ears. They always tumbled down when he boxed their ears, and they made a great fuss about it, and so finally his master was obliged to sell him to the showman. *His* name was Jinks.

"He taught my cousin several new tricks, and took him all over the country, exhibiting him in the different towns and villages. You see," said Bruin apologetically, "he—I mean Grimshaw—didn't know any better. He was so young when he was taken that he didn't remember much about his family, and didn't know what an undignified sort of thing it was to be going about in that way. One day, however, Jinks undertook to make him waltz with a piece of meat on his nose, without attempting to eat it. Grimshaw would not do that, because he didn't think it was reasonable; and I don't think it was. So then Jinks attempted to beat him, and Grimshaw boxed his ears, and he tumbled down and didn't get up again. Grimshaw waited a few minutes, and finding that he did not seem inclined to move, he ran away and took to the woods."

"But why did not the showman get up?" inquired the grandmother innocently.

"I think it highly probable that he was dead, madam," replied Bruin. "But I cannot say positively, as I was not there.

"After this Grimshaw lived alone for some time, wandering about from one forest to another. One day, as he was roaming up and down, he came suddenly upon a party of soldiers, three or four in number, sitting round a fire, and cooking their dinner. The moment they saw the bear, they dropped everything, and ran for their lives, leaving the good chops to burn, which was a sin. It was a good thing for Grimshaw, however, as he was very hungry; so he sat down by the fire and made a hearty meal. After he had dined comfortably, he began to look about him, and spied a big drum, which the soldiers had left behind in their flight. Seizing the drumsticks, he began to beat a lively tattoo. In a few moments he heard a rustling among the bushes, and saw a man's head thrust cautiously out. What was his delight to recognize his old master, Sergeant Shaw! He threw down the drumsticks and uttered a peculiar howl. It was answered by a shrill whistle, and in another moment Shaw and Grimshaw were in each other's arms. When the other soldiers ventured to return, they found the two gravely dancing a hornpipe, with great mutual satisfaction."

"Oh! how delightful!" exclaimed Toto. "And did they stay together after that?"

"They found the two dancing a hornpipe."

"No, that was impossible," replied the bear. "But they spent a couple of days together, and parted with the utmost good-will.

"After roaming about for some time longer, my cousin met some other bears, who invited him to join them. To their great amazement, one of them turned out to be Grimshaw's elder brother; he recognized Grimshaw by one of his ears, out of which he had himself bitten a piece in their infancy. This was a very joyful meeting, and led to the restoration of Grimshaw to his parents, who were still alive. He spent the remainder of his life in peace and happiness; and that is all there is to tell about him.

"And now," continued Bruin, "you ought to have been asleep long ago, Toto, and I have been keeping you awake with my long story. Off with you, now! And good-night to you too, dear madam. I will lie here in front of the fire; and if any creature, human or otherwise, comes to disturb the house during the night, I will attend to that creature!"

<h1 style="text-align:center">CHAPTER XIII.</h1>

THE grandmother thought, the next morning, that she had not passed such a pleasant evening, or such a comfortable and restful night, for a long time. "Dear me!" she said, after Bruin had departed, with many thanks and at least ten profound bows,—"dear me! what a difference it makes, having a bear in the house! one feels so secure; and one does not think of waking up to listen, every time a branch snaps outside, or a door creaks in the house. I wonder—" But the grandmother did not tell Toto what she wondered.

The next fine afternoon, the animals all came to the cottage in good season, for they were to have a story from their kind hostess herself this time, and it was to be about a giant.

"And if you will believe it," said the raccoon, "our poor Chucky here does not— ha! ha!—actually does not know what a giant is! Will you kindly explain to him, dear madam?"

"Ugh!" grunted the woodchuck. "I don't believe you know yourself, Coon, for all your airs! You said this morning it was a kind of vegetable, and now—"

"Stop quarrelling, and listen to the story, will you?" said Bruin. "Wow!"

When the bear said "Wow" in that manner, all the others knew it meant business; and as he lay down at the grandmother's feet, they all drew nearer, and were silent in expectation.

"A giant," said the grandmother, "is like a man, only very much bigger; very, *very* much bigger. The giant about whom I am going to tell you was one of the largest of his kind, being no less than fourteen miles high."

There was a general murmur of amazement.

"Fourteen miles high!" the old lady repeated. "His name was as short as he himself was long, for it was neither more nor less than *Crump*; and he fell in love with the Lady Moon. He fell so deeply in love with her that it was quite impossible for him to get out again; so he informed her of the fact, and begged her to marry him.

'Come and share my mammoth lot,

And shine in my gigantic cot!'

86

That was what he said, or words to that effect.

"But the Lady Moon replied, 'Dear Crump, I would gladly do as you suggest, but the thing is not possible. I have no body, but only a head; and I could not think of going into church to be married without any body, to say nothing of legs and feet.'

"'Is that your only objection?' asked Giant Crump.

"'The only one, upon my lunar honor!' replied the Lady Moon.

"'Then I think I can manage it,' said the giant. Accordingly he went and gathered together all the silver there was in the world at that time, and out of it he made a beautiful silver body, with arms and legs all complete. And when it was finished he made a silver dress, and silver slippers, and a silver moonshade, and dressed the body up in the most fashionable and delightful manner. Then, when all was ready, he called to the Lady Moon, and told her that her body was ready, and that she had only to come down and put it on.

"'But I cannot come down,' said the Lady Moon. 'Nothing would induce me to come down without a body. You must bring it up here.'

"Now that was not an easy thing to do; for though Crump was very big, he was not nearly big enough. What are fourteen miles, compared with two hundred and forty thousand? However, he was a very persevering giant, and had no idea of giving up; and he was very clever too. So he sat down on the ground and reflected for the space of seven years, and at the end of that time a thought struck him.

"He rose at once, and went to work and made a pair of stilts, high enough to reach to the moon. That was quite a piece of work, as you may imagine; but when they were finished, a new difficulty arose: how was he to get up on them? This required more reflection, and Crump sat and thought about it for six weeks more. Then another thought struck him, which was really an extremely clever one. He made a long ladder, as long as the stilts. He set this up against one of the stilts, and climbed up and put one foot on it; and then he set the ladder against the other stilt, and climbed up and put the other foot on that; this was very difficult, but it was also very clever. I forgot to say that he took the silver body up with him. Then he called out to the Lady Moon, 'Here I am, dear Lady Moon, and here is your silver body. Stop now, stop your rolling, and let me fasten it on for you, and then come down and be my beautiful silver bride.' And he held up the silver body, which shone and sparkled in the most enchanting manner.

"Here I am, dear Lady Moon."

"But the Lady Moon replied, 'Stop rolling, indeed! that is quite out of the question, I assure you. I have never done such a thing, and I am not going to begin at my time of life. No, no, Giant Crump; if you want me, you must catch me!' and she went rolling on in the most heartless and unfeeling way.

"There was nothing for the poor giant to do but follow; so, tucking the silver body under his arm, he set off on his tall stilts, and walked after the Lady Moon. Round and round the world went she, and round and round went the giant after her; and as I have never heard of his catching up with her, he is very likely walking round and round still."

"Is that all?" inquired the insatiable Toto. "What a very short story, Granny!"

"It is rather short," said the grandmother; "but I don't see how it could be made any longer. I will, however, if you wish, tell you another short story, and that will be equal to one long one. Listen, therefore, and you shall hear the story of Hokey Pokey."

So they listened, and heard it.

"Hokey Pokey was the youngest of a large family of children. His elder brothers, as they grew up, all became either butchers or bakers or makers of candlesticks, for such was the custom of the family. But Hokey Pokey would be none of these things; so when he was grown to be a tall youth he went to his father and said, 'Give me my fortune.'

"'Will you be a butcher?' asked his father.

"'No,' said Hokey Pokey.

"'Will you be a baker?'

"'No, again.'

"'Will you make candlesticks?'

"'Nor that either.'

"'Then,' said his father, 'this is the only fortune I can give you;' and with that he took up his cudgel and gave the youth a stout beating. 'Now you cannot complain that I gave you nothing,' said he.

"'That is true,' said Hokey Pokey. 'But give me also the wooden mallet which lies on the shelf, and I will make my way through the world.'

"His father gave him the mallet, glad to be so easily rid of him, and Hokey Pokey went out into the world to seek his fortune. He walked all day, and at nightfall he came to a small village. Feeling hungry, he went into a baker's shop, intending to buy a loaf of bread for his supper. There was a great noise and confusion in the back part of the shop; and on going to see what was the matter, he found the baker on his knees beside a large box or chest, which he was trying with might and main to keep shut. But there was something inside the box which was trying just as hard to get out, and it screamed and kicked, and pushed the lid up as often as the baker shut it down.

"'What have you there in the box?' asked Hokey Pokey.

"'I have my wife,' replied the baker. 'She is so frightfully ill-tempered that whenever I am going to bake bread I am obliged to shut her up in this box, lest she push me into the oven and bake me with the bread, as she has often threatened to do. But to-day she has broken the lock of the box, and I know not how to keep her down.'

"'That is easily managed,' said Hokey Pokey. 'Do you but tell her, when she asks who I am, that I am a giant with three heads, and all will be well.' So saying, he took his wooden mallet and dealt three tremendous blows on the box, saying in a loud voice,—

'Hickory Hox!

I sit by the box,

Waiting to give you a few of my knocks.

"'Husband, husband! whom have you there?' cried the wife in terror.

"'Alas!' said the baker; 'it is a frightful giant with three heads. He is sitting by the box, and if you open it so much as the width of your little finger, he will pull you out and beat you to powder.'

"When the wife heard that she crouched down in the box, and said never a word, for she was afraid of her life.

"The baker then took Hokey Pokey into the other part of the shop, thanked him warmly, and gave him a good supper and a bed. The next morning he gave him for a present the finest loaf of bread in his shop, which was shaped like a large round ball; and Hokey Pokey, after knocking once more on the lid of the box, continued his travels.

"He had not gone far before he came to another village, and wishing to inquire his way he entered the first shop he came to, which proved to be that of a confectioner. The shop was full of the most beautiful sweetmeats imaginable, and everything was bright and gay; but the confectioner himself sat upon a bench, weeping bitterly.

"'What ails you, friend?' asked Hokey-Pokey; 'and why do you weep, when you are surrounded by the most delightful things in the world?'

"'Alas!' replied the confectioner. 'That is just the cause of my trouble. The sweetmeats that I make are so good that their fame has spread far and wide, and the Rat King, hearing of them, has taken up his abode in my cellar. Every night he comes up and eats all the sweetmeats I have made the day before. There is no comfort in my life, and I am thinking of becoming a rope-maker and hanging myself with the first rope I make.'

"'Why don't you set a trap for him?' asked Hokey Pokey.

"'I have set fifty-nine traps,' replied the confectioner, 'but he is so strong that he breaks them all.'

"'Poison him,' suggested Hokey Pokey.

"'He dislikes poison,' said the confectioner, 'and will not take it in any form.'

"'In that case,' said Hokey Pokey, 'leave him to me. Go away, and hide yourself for a few minutes, and all will be well.'

"The confectioner thanked him warmly."

"The confectioner retired behind a large screen, having first showed Hokey Pokey the hole of the Rat King, which was certainly a very large one. Hokey

Pokey sat down by the hole, with his mallet in his hand, and said in a squeaking voice,—

'Ratly King! Kingly Rat!

Here your mate comes pit-a-pat.

Come and see; the way is free;

Hear my signal: one! two! three!'

And he scratched three times on the floor. Almost immediately the head of a rat popped up through the hole. He was a huge rat, quite as large as a cat; but his size was no help to him, for as soon as he appeared, Hokey Pokey dealt him such a blow with his mallet that he fell down dead without even a squeak. Then Hokey Pokey called the confectioner, who came out from behind the screen and thanked him warmly; he also bade him choose anything he liked in the shop, in payment for his services.

"'Can you match this?' asked Hokey Pokey, showing his round ball of bread.

"'That can I!' said the confectioner; and he brought out a most beautiful ball, twice as large as the loaf, composed of the finest sweetmeats in the world, red and yellow and white. Hokey Pokey took it with many thanks, and then went on his way.

"The next day he came to a third village, in the streets of which the people were all running to and fro in the wildest confusion.

"'What is the matter?' asked Hokey Pokey, as one man ran directly into his arms.

"'Alas!' replied the man. 'A wild bull has got into the principal china-shop, and is breaking all the beautiful dishes.'

"'Why do you not drive him out?' asked Hokey Pokey.

"'We are afraid to do that,' said the man; 'but we are running up and down to express our emotion and sympathy, and that is something.'

"'Show me the china-shop,' said Hokey Pokey.

"So the man showed him the china-shop; and there, sure enough, was a furious bull, making most terrible havoc. He was dancing up and down on a Dresden dinner set, and butting at the Chinese mandarins, and switching down finger-bowls and teapots with his tail, bellowing meanwhile in the most outrageous manner. The floor was covered with broken crockery, and the whole scene was melancholy to behold.

"Now when Hokey Pokey saw this, he said to the owner of the china-shop, who was tearing his hair in a frenzy of despair, 'Stop tearing your hair, which is indeed a senseless occupation, and I will manage this matter for you. Bring me a red cotton umbrella, and all will yet be well.'

"So the china-shop man brought him a red cotton umbrella, and Hokey Pokey began to open and shut it violently in front of the door. When the bull saw that, he stopped dancing on the Dresden dinner set and came charging out of the shop, straight towards the red umbrella. When he came near enough, Hokey Pokey dropped the umbrella, and raising his wooden mallet hit the bull such a blow on the muzzle that he fell down dead, and never bellowed again.

"The people all flung up their hats, and cheered, and ran up and down all the more, to express their gratification. As for the china-shop man, he threw his arms round Hokey Pokey's neck, called him his cherished preserver, and bade him choose anything that was left in his shop in payment for his services.

"'Can you match these?' asked Hokey Pokey, holding up the loaf of bread and the ball of sweetmeats.

"'That can I,' said the shop-man; and he brought out a huge ball of solid ivory, inlaid with gold and silver, and truly lovely to behold. It was very heavy, being twice as large as the ball of sweetmeats; but Hokey Pokey took it, and, after thanking the shop-man and receiving his thanks in return, he proceeded on his way.

"After walking for several days, he came to a fair, large castle, in front of which sat a man on horseback. When the man saw Hokey Pokey, he called out,—

"'Who are you, and what do you bring to the mighty Dragon, lord of this castle?'

"'Hokey Pokey is my name,' replied the youth, 'and strange things do I bring. But what does the mighty Dragon want, for example?'

"'He wants something new to eat,' said the man on horseback. 'He has eaten of everything that is known in the world, and pines for something new. He who brings him a new dish, never before tasted by him, shall have a thousand crowns and a new jacket; but he who fails, after three trials, shall have his jacket taken away from him, and his head cut off besides.'

"'I bring strange food,' said Hokey Pokey. 'Let me pass in, that I may serve the mighty Dragon.'

"Then the man on horseback lowered his lance, and let him pass in, and in short space he came before the mighty Dragon. The Dragon sat on a silver throne, with a golden knife in one hand, and a golden fork in the other. Around him were many people, who offered him dishes of every description; but he would none of them, for he had tasted them all before; and he howled with hunger on his silver throne. Then came forward Hokey Pokey, and said boldly,—

"'Here come I, Hokey Pokey, bringing strange food for the mighty Dragon.'

"The Dragon howled again, and waving his knife and fork, bade Hokey Pokey give the food to the attendants, that they might serve him.

"'Not so,' said Hokey Pokey. 'I must serve you myself, most mighty Dragon, else you shall not taste of my food. Therefore put down your knife and fork, and open your mouth, and you shall see what you shall see.'

"So the Dragon, after summoning the man-with-the-thousand-crowns and the man-with-the-new-jacket to one side of his throne, and the man-to-take-away-the-old-jacket and the executioner to the other, laid down his knife and fork and opened his mouth. Hokey Pokey stepped lightly forward, and dropped the round loaf down the great red throat. The Dragon shut his jaws together with a snap, and swallowed the loaf in two gulps.

"'That is good,' he said; 'but it is not new. I have eaten much bread, though never before in a round loaf. Have you anything more? Or shall the man take away your jacket?'

"'I have this, an it please you,' said Hokey Pokey; and he dropped the ball of sweetmeats into the Dragon's mouth.

"When the Dragon tasted this, he rolled his eyes round and round, and was speechless with delight for some time. At length he said, 'Worthy youth, this is very good; it is extremely good; it is better than anything I ever tasted. Nevertheless, it is not new; for I have tasted the same kind of thing before, only not nearly so good. And now, unless you are positively sure that you have something new for your third trial, you really might as well take off your jacket; and the executioner shall take off your head at the same time, as it is getting rather late. Executioner, do your—'

"People," he said, "I am Hokey Pokey."

"'Craving your pardon, most mighty Dragon,' said Hokey Pokey, 'I will first make my third trial;' and with that he dropped the ivory ball into the Dragon's mouth.

"'Gug-wugg-gllll-grrr!' said the Dragon, for the ball had stuck fast, being too big for him to swallow.

"Then Hokey Pokey lifted his mallet and struck one tremendous blow upon the ball, driving it far down the throat of the monster, and killing him most fatally dead. He rolled off the throne like a scaly log, and his crown fell off and rolled to Hokey Pokey's feet. The youth picked it up and put it on his own head, and then called the people about him and addressed them.

"'People,' he said, 'I am Hokey Pokey, and I have come from a far land to rule over you. Your Dragon have I slain, and now I am your king; and if you will always do exactly what I tell you to do, you will have no further trouble.'

"So the people threw up their caps and cried, 'Long live Hokey Pokey!' and they always did exactly as he told them, and had no further trouble.

"And Hokey Pokey sent for his three brothers, and made them Chief Butcher, Chief Baker, and Chief Candlestick-maker of his kingdom. But to his father he sent a large cudgel made of pure gold, with these words engraved on it: 'Now you cannot complain that I have given you nothing!'"

CHAPTER XIV

"YA-Ha!" said the raccoon, yawning and stretching himself. "Ya-a-*hoo*! Hm-a-yeaow! oh, dear me! what a pity!"

"What, for instance, is the matter?" demanded the squirrel, dropping a hickory-nut down on the raccoon's nose. "I knew a raccoon once who yawned till his head broke in two, and the top rolled off."

"Hm!" said the raccoon. "Not much loss if it was like some people's heads.

"I was sighing," he continued, "you very stupid Cracker! to think that summer is gone, and that winter will be here before we can say 'Beechnuts.'"

"Ah!" said the squirrel, looking grave. "That, indeed! To be sure; yes."

"The leaves are falling fast," continued the raccoon meditatively; "the birds are all gone, except Pigeon Pretty and Miss Mary, and they are going in a day or two. Very soon, my Cracker, we shall have to roll ourselves up and go to sleep for the winter. No more gingerbread and jam, my boy. No more pleasant afternoons at the cottage; no more stories. Nothing but a hollow tree and four months' sleep. Ah, dear me!" and Coon sighed again, and shook his head despondingly.

"By the way," said Cracker, "Toto tells me that he and his people don't sleep in winter any more than in summer. Queer, isn't it? I suppose it has something to do with their having only two legs."

"Something to do with their having two heads!" growled the raccoon. "They don't sleep with their legs, do they, stupid?"

"They certainly don't sleep *without* them!" said the squirrel rather sharply.

"Look here!" replied the raccoon, rising and shaking himself, "should you like me to bite about two inches off your tail? It won't take me a minute, and I would just as lief do it as not."

Affairs were becoming rather serious, when suddenly the wood-pigeon appeared, and fluttered down with a gentle "Coo!" between the two friends, who certainly seemed anything but friendly.

"What are you two quarrelling about?" she asked. "How extremely silly you both are! But now make friends, and put on your very best manners, for we are going to have a visitor here in a few minutes. I am going to call Chucky and Miss Mary, and do you make everything tidy about the pool before she comes." And off flew Pigeon Pretty in a great hurry.

"*She?*" said Cracker inquiringly, looking at Coon.

"She *said* 'she'!" replied Coon, bestirring himself, and picking up the dead branches that had fallen on the smooth green moss-carpet.

"Perhaps it is that aunt of Chucky's who has been making him a visit," suggested the squirrel.

"Oh, well!" said the raccoon, stopping short in his work. "If Pigeon Pretty thinks I am going to put this place in order for a woodchuck's aunt, she is very much mistaken, that's all. I never heard of such—" But here he stopped, for a loud rustling in the underbrush announced that the visitor, whoever she might be, was close at hand.

The bushes separated, and to the utter astonishment of both Coon and Cracker, who should appear but the grandmother herself, escorted by Toto and Bruin, and attended also by the wood-pigeon and the parrot, who fluttered about her head with cries of pleasure.

Toto led the old lady to the mossy bank beside the pool, where she sat down, rather out of breath, and a little bewildered, but evidently much pleased at having accomplished such a feat.

The raccoon hastened to express his delight in the finest possible language, while the little squirrel turned a dozen somersaults in succession, by way of showing how pleased he was. As for the worthy Bruin, he fairly beamed with pleasure, and even went so far as to execute a sort of saraband, which, if the grandmother could have seen it, would certainly have alarmed her a good deal.

"My dear friends," said the old lady, "it gives me great pleasure to be here, I assure you. Toto has for some time had his heart quite set on my seeing you once—though, alas! my *seeing* is only *hearing*—in your own pleasant home, before you separate for the winter. So, thanks to our kind friend, Mr. Bruin, I am actually here. How warm and soft the air is!" she continued. "What a delightful cushion you have found for me! and is that a brook, that is tinkling so pleasantly?"

"That is the spring, Granny!" said Toto eagerly. "It bubbles up, as clear as crystal, out of a hole in the rock, and then it falls over into the pool. And the pool is round, as round as a cup; and there are ferns and purple flags growing all around it, and the trees are all reflected in it, you know; and there are turtles in it, and there used to be a muskrat, only Coon ate him, and—and—oh! it's so jolly!" and here Toto paused, fairly out of breath.

Indeed, it was very lovely by the pool, in the soft glow of the Indian summer day. The spring murmured and tinkled and sang to them; the trees dropped yellow leaves on them, like fairy gold; and then the sun laughed, and sent down flights of his golden arrows, to show them what a very poor thing earthly gold was, after all. So they all sat and talked around the pool, of the summer that was past and the winter that was coming. Then the grandmother made a little speech which she had been thinking over for some time. It was a very short speech; but it was very much to the point.

"Dear friends," she said, "you are all sad at the prospect of the long winter; but I have a plan which will make the winter a joyous season, instead of a melancholy one. I have plenty of room in my cottage, warmth, and food, and everything comfortable; and I want you all to come and spend the winter with Toto and me. There is a large wood-pile where you can climb or sit when you are tired of the house. You shall sleep when you please, and wake when you please; and we will be a happy and united family. Come, my friends, what do you say?"

"Then the grandmother made a little speech."

What did they say? Indeed, they did not know what to say. There was silence around the pool for a few minutes. Then the bear looked at the raccoon, the raccoon looked at the squirrel, and the squirrel looked at the wood-pigeon; and finally the gentle bird answered, as she usually did, for all.

"Dear, dear madam," she said, "we can imagine nothing so delightful as to live with you and our dear Toto. We all accept your invitation thankfully and joyfully; and we will all do our best to be a help, rather than a burden, to you."

All the animals nodded approval. Then Toto, who had been waiting breathless for the answer, seized the bear by the paws, and the raccoon seized the squirrel, and they all danced round and round till there was no breath left in their bodies; and the woodchuck—who had been asleep behind a tree, and had waked up just in time to hear the grandmother's speech—danced all alone on his hind-legs, to the admiration of all beholders. And then Cracker went and brought some nuts, and Coon brought apples, and Bruin brought great shining combs of honey, and they sat and feasted around the pool, and were right merry.

And then they all went back to the cottage,—the grandmother, and Toto, and Bruin, and Coon, and Cracker, and Chucky, and Pigeon Pretty, and Miss Mary,—and there they all lived and were happy; and if you ever lead half such a merry life as they did, you may consider yourself extremely fortunate.

THE END